RAINBOW WISHES

Jacqueline Case

A KISMET™ Romance

METEOR PUBLISHING CORPORATION
Bensalem, Pennsylvania

To my mother, my friend.
For believing in me when even *I* didn't.

JACQUELINE CASE

Jacqueline Case lives in the town where she was born, just outside Portland, Oregon. She is "thirtysomething," and still looking for Mr. Right. (Please, don't tell me the odds against finding him after the age of thirty. We hopeful romantics pay no attention to such statistics!) Jacqueline divides her time between a full time job, housework and writing. Sometimes she even fits some sleep into her schedule.

ONE

Frigid wind danced around Evie Winthrop's creeping car, whipping the heavily falling snow into a shifting, undulating curtain of white that obscured the road before her. What had been no more than a light snowfall in Seattle had turned into a full-fledged blizzard as she approached the summit of Steven's Pass, deep in central Washington's Wenatchee National Forest.

Evie's hands tightened on the steering wheel as a potent gust of wind buffeted the car, causing it to skid on the snow-slicked road. She was miles from her home in Leavenworth—or from anywhere else, for that matter. Not a single car had gone by for the past hour. At this time of year few drivers wanted to attempt the trip at night, even under the best of conditions.

She really shouldn't have tried it herself, she admitted reluctantly, but December was already upon them. Her restaurant had to be prepared for the crowds that would gather in the little village where she lived to take part in their annual Christmas Lighting Festival.

When the printing house in Seattle had informed her of an outrageously large increase in their delivery charges for her holiday placemats and napkins, she had decided to take matters into her own hands. She had driven to Seattle early that morning and picked up the order herself.

And where had it gotten her? Caught in the middle of a blizzard, that's where, she thought bitterly. Great. Just simply great. So she'd managed to hold her own in the world of business. Maybe she would find that more comforting if she were at home in front of her own fireplace tonight instead of fighting this nerve-wracking battle against the elements.

Another gust of wind, stronger than the last, hit the side of the car, sending it skidding across the narrow, two-lane highway. Adrenaline surged through her body as she struggled vainly for control. The car spun around, heading blindly off the road. When it came to a stop, it was nosed into a ditch, almost hidden from the road.

Evie sat there for a moment, stunned by the jolting stop but uninjured. From the sharp downward angle of the car, she knew at once that there was no way she could get it back up on the highway. Reaction set in, and she began to tremble violently.

The wind howled loudly, and it was a moment before she noticed that the engine was no longer running. It had stalled out.

She turned the key in the ignition with fingers

that shook. Nothing. She tried again, and yet again before she allowed herself to accept the truth. The faulty starter that had been such a source of annoyance to her had taken on a new significance. Her only source of heat until rescuers arrived was gone.

Chill fingers of panic ran along her spine, but she forced them back. She fumbled for her thermos of hot coffee and shook it. It was almost empty, she realized. After switching on her emergency flashers, she reached for the blanket that she always carried with her for wintertime trips and wrapped herself in it to conserve her body heat while she waited for help to arrive.

Evie worried that she was not well enough prepared to face a night in this storm. When she had left home, the weather had been unusually mild. She foolishly had wanted to impress the people she was doing business with, and had worn a tailored blue wool business suit, instead of her usual jeans and sweater.

Her shapely legs were covered only by sheer, smoky-colored nylons, and her feet were clad in stylish but totally impractical suede pumps. She silently cursed her lack of foresight.

Still, she *was* on the main highway, she thought, trying to comfort herself. Eventually someone was bound to come along and see her lights. She curled up in the blanket, settling back to wait. She only hoped that help would arrive before the freezing temperatures took their toll.

It was the first vacation Mason Kincaid had taken in years, and he was already sorry he had allowed himself to be talked into it. His battered old pickup was having a tough time making it through the blizzard, and more miles than he wanted to think about still separated him from the comfort of his friend's vacation home.

At thirty-four years of age, Mase told himself that he was far too young to be experiencing a mid-life crisis, but deep down inside, he wondered. Of course, the news of Gramps's death had come as a blow to him. The older man had been the only family Mase had known since he had gone to live with him as a troubled teenager. No one else, including his parents, had cared what became of him.

His career in the Army had not allowed him to be close to Gramps in recent years, but since he'd died, Mase had been conscious of a void in his life. He had impulsively decided to resign his commission and make a life for himself in the civilian world.

When he had informed his colonel of his decision, the understanding older man had advised him to take some time off and consider his decision carefully. After all, he had been in the Army for sixteen years. He shouldn't jump into anything. Since he had a great deal of leave coming, Mase had taken that advice, as well as the offer of a friend's cabin for a ski vacation.

Flashing red lights drew his eyes to the side of the highway. When he eased carefully to a stop, his headlights illuminated the rear end of a car that was almost buried by the snow.

Mase pulled on his ski cap and reached into the

unlit glove box, his cold fingers fumbling for a flashlight. He had more difficulty than he expected as he tried to get down the slope to reach the door of the car. There was no response to his knock on the window, so he shined the flashlight beam inside.

His heart skipped a beat when he saw the blanket-wrapped figure of a woman slumped behind the wheel. How long had she been out here, he wondered? Even a few hours could be too long in an unheated car. He tried the door, but found it locked.

Without hesitating, he moved down to the rear passenger window. After glancing inside to be sure that no one sat there, he took the heavy metal flashlight and hit the frozen glass with all the power of his tough, muscular body. He had to strike at it several times until enough shards of broken glass came away to allow him to get his hand inside to pull up the lock.

When he eased the door open, the slight form within the blanket stirred, and the woman murmured something so softly that he could not understand. A wave of relief flooded through him. At least she was still alive. As Mase knew only too well, hypothermia was a dangerous adversary. He had fallen victim to it once himself, while on maneuvers. It numbed the mind as well as the body, and that was an experience one didn't forget.

He eased her out from behind the wheel, trying to keep the blanket wrapped snugly around her. Mase was bracing her against his chest preparing to lift her into his arms when her body grew unexpectedly tense.

When she started to fight him, his arms tightened instinctively around her. He was surprised by her strength, but the heavy blanket which enveloped her hampered her struggles.

As she fought him, Mase's booted foot, which was braced in the heavy snow, slid, throwing him off balance. A moment later they both landed heavily on the ground, his big body pressing hers deeply into the snow.

The shock of the fall seemed to jar her back to rationality, and Mase was relieved to see a glimmering of intelligence and growing awareness in her face.

"Are you all right?" he asked, willing her to respond.

"I'm not sure," she said dazedly. "What happened?"

"Your car went off the road," he replied gently. "I don't know how long you've been here. I just happened to find you as I drove by. Have you been hurt? We need to get you out of this cold, but I don't want to move you if you've been injured."

"I think I may have twisted my bad knee," she admitted reluctantly. "I injured it several years ago in . . . in an accident and it's still not very strong."

"Which knee?" he asked.

"The left."

He levered himself up off her, and helped her to a sitting position. After stripping off his gloves, he braced her back against the wheel of her car.

She started in surprise as his large, warm hands closed around her leg, gently straightening the injured limb.

"It's all right," he said softly. "I'll be careful. I won't hurt you."

His hard fingers probed gingerly at the tender, slightly swollen flesh, searching for injuries. Evie's breath caught in her throat and she stiffened instinctively.

"Well, at least it doesn't seem to be broken," he said. "We'd better try to get you into my truck. You're cold already, and hypothermia is nothing to fool around with."

He pushed the snow-covered blanket aside, abandoning it to the cold forest. The last thing this woman needed was to be wrapped in the wetness of that blanket after the snow melted.

A brawny arm encircled her slender shoulders and another slipped beneath her thighs. The wispy nylon fabric of her stockings was no protection against the rough wool of his jacket. The prickly material rubbing against her delicate flesh sent a shiver the length of her body that she only hoped he would attribute to the cold. If only she could think more clearly.

Her weight did not seem to encumber him in the slightest as he cradled her snugly against his broad chest and carried her to the pickup. He settled her on the passenger side of the high seat with great care.

A moment later, he climbed in the other door and started the engine. Evie heaved a soft sigh of relief, leaning her spinning head against the side window. Her breath made patterns on the cold glass. It was wonderful to be inside and away from the frigid wind and blowing snow. Slowly, her thoughts began to clear.

"I'm afraid the heater isn't working," he apologized as he reached behind the seat. With a small sound of satisfaction, he pulled out a heavy wool blanket and tucked it around her. "This should help some, though," he continued, cupping his gloved hands together and blowing into the hollow to warm them. "How much farther is it to Leavenworth? The signs have been so covered with snow that I haven't been able to read them."

"It's almost twenty miles," Evie replied, turning toward him as he started the engine and eased the truck back out onto the highway.

"That far?" he asked in disappointment.

"I have an idea, that is, if you aren't determined to go all the way to Leavenworth tonight," she said, studying him from under her lashes.

"What do you have in mind?" he asked, glancing over at her.

"My aunt and uncle live near here. That's where I was heading. It's probably not more than a mile to the turn-off to their house. It's set in about a half mile from the highway, but the driving couldn't be much worse than this."

"That's for sure," he agreed. "I'm game to try it. Oh, by the way," he added, "my name is Mason Kincaid. Mase to my friends."

"I'm Evie Winthrop," she responded, clenching her teeth in an effort to keep them from chattering.

"Pleased to meet you, Evie Winthrop," he said, a smile transforming his face, softening the harsh planes with a hint of humor.

"I don't see why you should be," she returned, an answering smile curving her lips. "I've caused you a lot of trouble. Thanks for helping me. I don't want to think of what would have happened if you hadn't stopped."

"No problem. It isn't often that a man has the chance to rescue a lady in distress these days," he replied with a gleam in his eyes.

A tremor started at the base of her neck, rippling down across her shoulders and all through her slight frame as her body tried in vain to warm itself. A second tremor shook her, followed by a third, and then a fourth. Evie huddled deeper into the heavy folds of the blanket, seeking warmth that wasn't there.

"Are you sure you're all right?" he asked again.

Mase was surprised by his concern for the shivering girl beside him. It had been a long time since a woman had aroused his protective urges the way she had.

"Yes. I'm j-just cold. I'll warm up soon," she lied. Actually Evie doubted if anything short of a scalding-hot two-hour bath could warm her up again.

The silence stretched out painfully, putting a further strain on her tense nerves. She was all too aware of the man beside her. He seemed to surround her, filling the small cab of the pickup. His breath misted against the frozen windshield, and the masculine smell of his woodsy cologne mingled with his body's natural musky scent, creating a pleasantly heady fragrance.

Evie hoped she had done the right thing in going with this unknown man. She hadn't had a lot of options. It had come down to a choice between the storm and Mason Kincaid.

She studied his face in the strange half-light peculiar to snowy nights, committing the angular features to memory. She saw the strength and determination there, and it reassured her. This man could handle anything nature dished out. For the time being, she would be content with that.

Evie was as familiar with the turn-off to her uncle's house as she was with the back of her hand, but she still didn't see the tall yellow snow marker until they had already passed it by.

"There," she said. "We just passed it on the right."

Mase eased the truck around, making a U-turn in the middle of the highway. They entered the hidden road at a slow crawl.

They actually found the driving easier on the narrow road than it had been on the open highway. Huge trees surrounded the drive and sheltered it from the elements. It was rather like driving through a snow tunnel, Evie thought, shut off from the vastness of the snowy night. In that moment they might have been the only two people on earth. It was a disquieting idea in more ways than one.

Finally they entered the semicircular approach

to the house. To Evie's surprise and increasing confusion, the house was in complete darkness.

"They couldn't have gone to bed already," she said. "It isn't even eight o'clock."

"Maybe the electricity is out," Mase suggested.

"But they're prepared for that. If the power was out, they'd have lit kerosene lamps. They must not be home. Maybe they drove into town before the weather turned bad. I hope they're all right."

"What do you want to do?" Mase asked, leaving the decision up to her.

"We really don't have much choice. We can't go any farther tonight. I know where the spare key is hidden. I'm sure they'd want us to stay."

"Okay," he agreed with relief. "You probably shouldn't be up and around on that leg any more than you have to. Tell me where the key is, and I'll open the door."

"It's attached to the underside of a loose board on the porch, up against the house on the left side of the wood box," Evie told him.

He fumbled in the unlit glove box for a flashlight before opening the door and stepping out into the blizzard. Within seconds he had vanished from sight.

Evie was strangely uneasy as she stared out into the night by herself. She knew it was foolish. Even if she couldn't see him, Mase was only a few steps away. Besides, she barely knew the man. If she had any sense at all, she would be more nervous when he was there than when he was gone.

The thought of leaning on someone else's

strength was enticing. All her life Evie'd had no one but herself to depend on. But it wouldn't do to start depending on Mase. When the storm ended, she would never see him again, and she had better remember that.

Like a ghost stepping out of the dark, snowy night, Mase appeared once again. When he opened the car door, Evie turned and looked up at him.

"It's open," he said, slipping an arm under her legs and scooting her toward him. "Let's get inside."

Mase lifted her into his arms once again, covering the short distance to the porch through the icy, white world with the sure-footed grace of a powerful cat. Once inside, he kicked the door shut behind him and paused to get his bearings in the dark, still house.

A few steps took them to the doorway of the living room where he paused once again, fumbling for a light switch. He found it, but flipped it in vain.

"Looks like the electricity *is* out," he said unnecessarily. "Take the flashlight out of my coat pocket for me, would you?"

Evie uncurled one arm from around his strong neck and worked her hand between their bodies, down into his pocket. Her body hummed with awareness of the rock-hard muscles beneath his coat and the rise and fall of his chest against hers.

Her fumbling fingers found the cold metal stem at last. She slipped it out, snapping it on to shine a bright white beam across the dark room.

Mase followed its path and discovered the large

couch in the middle of the room. He carried Evie over and settled her at one end with her injured leg stretched out before he turned to survey the rest of the room.

"There are two kerosene lamps on the mantel," Evie said. Her voice seemed unnaturally loud in the large, silent room.

The beam swung around, seeking the lamps. He moved across the floor to the massive stone fireplace, and moments later the light of the twin lamps bathed the homey room in a golden glow.

It was an attractive room, warm and casual and infinitely comfortable. The twelve-foot high-beamed ceiling and stone fireplace gave it a rustic look. It was the kind of room that had known the laughter and clutter of children at play. Evie had daydreamed about a home like this when she was a child living a hard, lonely life in a succession of cheap rental houses with her mother and stepfather.

She had loved this house from the first moment she had set eyes on it. She had been a frightened, homeless girl of twelve then, alone and hungry for love.

She had found the sense of belonging there that she'd yearned for all her life. Although she now had her own comfortable little apartment in town, this would always be home to her.

"It's as cold in here as it was out in the pickup," Mase commented, breaking the silence.

"The electricity must have been off all day," Evie said, her teeth chattering as the chills continued to wrack her body.

Mase's bottle-green eyes narrowed, studying her small, trembling form. She was the picture of abject misery as she sat huddled under the chilly folds of the blanket, but she had not uttered a single word of complaint. In Mase's experience of women, that alone was enough to make Evie unique.

"Well, I'll get a fire started and it will be warm in here before you know it."

A few minutes later Mase dusted his hands on his powerful jeans-clad thighs, standing back to eye his handiwork with satisfaction. A cheery fire crackled on the hearth, casting a warm, orangy glow across the faded carpet. Heat wafted out into the room, and it immediately seemed cozy.

He shrugged his jacket off broad shoulders and threw it casually into a chair. His long legs carried him across the room in three strides, and as he bent over Evie, his muscular frame blocked out the warmth and light from the fire.

Evie felt uneasy. She was aware of the restrained power in the strong hands and arms which enfolded her, gathering her against him once again. That was the only thing that kept her uneasiness from blossoming into fear.

Mase carried her several steps closer to the heat of the fire, setting her down on a soft armchair and bracing her injured leg on the matching ottoman. He tugged the blanket off her shoulders and let it fall to the floor.

When he started to unbutton her coat, Evie shrank back into the cushions. He was startled when he looked up into silver-gray eyes that were wide with alarm.

"You'll be warmer without your coat, Evie," he said, his voice carefully matter-of-fact. "It's not really keeping you warm now. It's so cold and damp that it's keeping the heat out.

"Don't be afraid of me. We're stuck here together until the storm is over, so we might as well make the best of it, okay?"

"Okay," she murmured, her eyes meeting his for a brief moment before they dropped to her lap to hide her embarrassment. He must think she was a complete fool.

"I don't know about you, but I'm starved," Mase said. "I skipped dinner because I was in a hurry to get to Leavenworth."

"I'm hungry, too," she admitted.

"Well, then I guess there's only one thing keeping us from eating."

"What's that?" she inquired.

"I don't know where the kitchen is. If you tell me, I'll see if I can rustle something up."

"Sorry," she smiled feebly. "It's behind the stairway in the entry hall. There's a gas stove there, and my aunt usually keeps the cupboards well stocked in case of storms like this, so it shouldn't be hard to find something."

"I'll be right back," Mase promised, giving her an encouraging smile. He picked up one of the lamps on his way out of the room.

Evie closed her eyes and settled back into the softness of the old, overstuffed chair. Under the comforting warmth of the fire, the tremors that shook her body began to diminish, coming at ever longer intervals.

Mason Kincaid was an attractive man, she thought. His face was rather rugged, and some people might not consider him handsome at all, but Evie thought it suited his body. He was six feet four if he was an inch, and his frame was correspondingly broad and sturdy, covered with a hard wall of muscle. Unruly brown hair and deep green eyes completed a very attractive and some-what mysterious picture.

A slight movement caught Evie's attention, and she glanced around to find Mase standing at her side. She wondered briefly why the air of mystery added to his allure.

"Here, drink this," he said, offering her a small glass of dark amber liquid.

She took it automatically and stared into its depths as the soft light of the fire imbued it with a deep, rich glow.

"It's just brandy," he said, misinterpreting her hesitation. "I found a bottle in the kitchen cup-board. Go ahead and drink it. You might not like the taste, but it will warm you up."

Evie was too tired to argue, as he half expected her to do. She raised the glass to her lips and took a healthy sip.

To Mase's surprise, she did not gasp and cough over its strong, pungent taste. She sipped the expensive brandy with a blissful expression on her face that made him raise an eyebrow. It took expe-rience to drink brandy with that kind of ease, a type of experience that he had not given her credit for possessing.

A soft flush brought color to her pale cheeks, warming her thoroughly and banishing the last of her chills. She welcomed that warmth gratefully. Her breathing grew deeper and steadier, and as she leaned back into the corner of the chair, her breasts pressed against the sheer fabric of her blouse.

"I'll see about some supper," Mase said, dragging his eyes back to her face.

A combination of the brandy and the penetrating warmth of the fire made her drowsy, and Evie dozed as Mase prepared their meal. When he returned to the room, he studied her gently curving form for several moments before clearing his throat to alert her to his presence.

"Umm, that smells good," she said, her eyelids fluttering sleepily as he settled the tray on her lap.

"Well, I'm not exactly hell on wheels in the kitchen," he confessed with a boyish grin that surprised her. "But you can't do too much damage to tomato soup and grilled cheese sandwiches."

They sipped mugs of hot soup and nibbled the sizzling sandwiches slowly and in silence, but the silence was no longer uncomfortable. When they were done, Mase cleared away the trays, soaking the dirty dishes in cold water.

It was barely ten o'clock when he finished, but Evie was exhausted. The nerve-wracking evening combined with the nagging pain of her injured knee had drained her usually inexhaustible supply of energy.

Mase seemed tired, too. He must have been as worn-out as she was from the long hours of concentrated driving. It wasn't easy to fight the slippery, snowy roads for hours on end, she thought.

"Maybe we should turn in," he suggested. "We could both use a good night's sleep, but I think we'd better stay close to the fire. If you tell me where to find some blankets, I'll see what I can fix up."

A few minutes later Mase stood before her, surveying the room with his arms laden with blankets and pillows.

"I'll make up the couch for you, and I'll sleep on the floor in front of the fire," he said at last.

"That doesn't seem fair," she objected. "Why should I have the couch while you have to sleep on the hard floor?"

"I don't mind. The couch wouldn't be big enough for me anyway."

Evie recognized the truth of his statement and didn't argue further. When he had finished making up the beds, she stood and started to hobble across the room.

He cast her an exasperated look, crossing the room quickly to swing her up in his arms and deposit her on top of the couch.

"Uh . . . thank you," she murmured, climbing self-consciously under the covers.

Under the protection of the heavy blankets, Evie tried unobtrusively to work her pantyhose down over her injured knee. Comfortable or not, she would sleep in the remainder of her clothing. She couldn't bring herself to strip any further with Mase in the room.

Mase had no such scruples. After making his bed and turning out the kerosene lamps, he stood in front of the fire, stripping off his sweater, shirt, and pants as he prepared for bed.

Evie was amazed by her temerity as she watched him from under her lashes. She unpinned the coil of her long, dark hair and combed through it absently with her fingers. She was embarrassed, but at the same time fascinated by the large, masculine body which was silhouetted by the glow of the fire.

He did not make Evie quite so nervous now. Perhaps it was because he no longer reminded her of the man who haunted her dreams. *He* had been tall and broad, too, but the heavy bulk of his body had been soft and flabby. Evie knew from firsthand experience that Mase's body was all hard, lean muscle.

She remembered how pleasant his muscular chest had felt as she'd searched his pocket for the flashlight. An unfamiliar sense of yearning swept through her body, settling in her abdomen and moving lower. What was there about this man that inspired such feelings?

He was attractive, but Evie had known men who were far more handsome, including her former fiancé. Those men had never inspired the feelings she was experiencing now. Surely it was just a momentary aberration. In the morning when she was well rested, this would all be like a strange dream.

"Good night, Mase," she whispered, snuggling her cheek into the plump, downy pillow. "Thank you."

"Good night, Evie," he answered.

She closed her eyes and tried to compose herself for sleep. She fully expected to lie awake for hours, but moments later, she was asleep.

The soft, whimpering noises Evie had been making in her sleep caused Mase to stir. When the scream tore loose, as if making its way from the depths of her soul, he was jolted to instant awareness. Within seconds, he was at her side.

A nightmare, he realized in relief. He gripped her shoulders firmly and gave her a shake.

"Evie, wake up," he demanded.

Her eyes popped open, and Mase was stunned by the expression of sheer terror he found in their stormy gray depths. All at once, she began to fight.

Evie's strength, which was born of fear, took him by surprise, and for a moment, he was hard pressed to hold her. In the end he was forced to use the heavy bulk of his huge body to suppress her struggles, lying on top of her, her slim legs trapped between his muscular ones, her arms stretched taut above her head.

"Evie, wake up," he commanded in a voice that brooked no disobedience.

Her body went still beneath his, and her eyes grew wide with a combination of surprise and remembered fear. She was all too conscious of his big body stretched over hers, forcing her into submission. A tremor shook her.

Mase saw her fear and muttered a curse under his breath, sliding off her to sit on the floor. Evie curled up into a ball, oblivious to the pain from her injured knee. She hugged the pillow tightly.

"Are you all right?" he asked at length.

"Yes," she said, so softly that he could barely hear her. "It was just the nightmare."

The nightmare, he wondered? So she had a recurring nightmare, did she?

"Can I get you something?" he offered.

"No thanks. I'll be fine. I'm sorry I woke you."

Mase went back to his own bed before the fire and listened to Evie toss and turn. He had never seen such a look of terror on another human being's face. What could she be dreaming about that could frighten her so badly?

It was a long time before either of them slept again.

TWO

The fire had burned out during the night, and when Evie awoke the next morning, the room had grown cold. She savored the warmth of her little haven beneath the blankets, stretching cautiously to test her knee. To her relief, only a twinge of pain answered the movement when she flexed the injured joint.

She turned to glance at Mase, and found him deeply lost to sleep. It was several minutes before she could convince herself to leave that comforting warmth to make her way to the stairs, weighted down by the heavy blanket she clutched around her.

The small yellow bathroom upstairs was very cold, and Evie hurried through her morning ritual. After brushing her teeth and washing off the remains of yesterday's makeup, she felt almost human again. She worked the snarls out of her dark hair and fashioned it into a thick braid which reached halfway down her back.

She paused and contemplated the face that

stared back at her from the mirror. There was nothing unattractive about her face, but she had never thought of herself as being pretty. When she was younger, she had often wished for a slim, aquiline nose and dramatic, high cheekbones in place of her own, more commonplace features.

In her opinion, her best feature was her eyes. Fringed with long, dark lashes, they changed in color from bright silver to dark, stormy gray depending on her mood.

She shrugged and went on to the more important task of finding something to wear.

That proved to be simple, for both Evie and her aunt Janet were petite women. She chose the loosest, most comfortable jeans her aunt owned. They fit well enough, but hugged her thighs and derriere a bit more snugly than Evie would have liked.

Her ensemble was completed with a blue-and-gray plaid flannel shirt. Evie would have preferred the warmth of a sweater, but they were all too tight, emphasizing rather than concealing her ample curves.

Her stocking feet padded noiselessly down the stairs as she headed for the kitchen. Moving through the well-equipped room with the efficiency that came from years of practice, she lit the stove, put on a pot of coffee, and started breakfast. Diced potatoes sizzled alongside fragrant strips of bacon when Mase entered the kitchen a few minutes later.

"Umm, that smells great. I think I've died and gone to heaven," he said, inhaling deeply of the heady, breakfasty scent.

"Good morning," Evie said a bit shyly, continuing to scramble the eggs she had cracked into her bowl.

"Good morning. Anything I can do to help?" he asked, running his fingers through sleep-tousled hair.

"No thanks. I've got everything under control," she replied. "I set out a toothbrush and razor in the bathroom upstairs. You should have plenty of time to freshen up before breakfast is ready."

"That's the best offer I've had all day," he said, turning to go. "I won't be long."

Mase returned a few minutes later with his hair neatly combed, his jaw freshly shaven, and smelling invitingly of soap, minty toothpaste, and the musky scent of man.

"I hope you were able to go back to sleep last night," she said, broaching the subject in spite of her embarrassment. "I'm sorry I woke you."

"No problem," he replied, casually dismissing the subject. Evie was only too glad to let it drop.

She was aware of his eyes upon her as they filled their plates and carried them back to the living room. She wished vehemently that the snug jeans did not emphasize her rounded, womanly hips quite so much.

"Are you sure your aunt and uncle won't mind our moving in and making ourselves at home this way?"

"I'm sure," she replied, certain of that, at least. "I grew up in this house. I just moved away a few years ago when I went to school in Seattle. My aunt and uncle have been like parents to me."

"Have you lived with them all your life?"

"Since I was twelve. I lived with my mother and stepfather before that. We traveled all around the southern United States. We never stayed long in one place.

"The storm doesn't seem any better this morning, does it?" she went on awkwardly. "I wonder how much longer it will last."

"I couldn't say. I'm not too familiar with your weather in these parts. Basically, I'm a city boy."

"Actually there isn't much of any way to predict what these winter storms will do," she admitted. "Unless things change awfully fast, though, I'm afraid we'll have to resign ourselves to staying here a few more days."

"Things could be a lot worse," Mase reminded her. "At least we're warm and comfortable here."

"I know, but I have responsibilities back in town."

"I didn't think about that," he said, sounding displeased by the thought. "I suppose you have someone who will be worried about you."

"There's only my two employees, Ben and Liesel," she replied, oblivious to his meaning. "I just hope Liesel doesn't panic when I don't get home and call the sheriff."

Mase considered her guileless response. It was obvious that there was no particular man in her life. If any other woman of his acquaintance had made that statement, he would have taken it as an open invitation, but with Evie, he didn't know what to think.

When they finished their breakfast, Mase adjusted the half-burnt logs with a heavy poker, and flames curled responsively around them. It appeared that this city boy had experience with fireplaces. Evie's curiosity about him grew.

She went out to the kitchen to refill their coffee cups and put a large kettle of water on the stove to heat. With that task accomplished, she hurried back to the warmth of the living room.

"Thanks," Mase said as she handed him his cup. "It looks like your knee is doing all right today. At least you're not limping."

"It feels fine this morning. I was really lucky. Sometimes when I have trouble, it will last for days."

"We're getting pretty low on wood," he observed, rising from his chair before the fire and draining his cup. "I think I'll go bring in some more. Where is it?"

"It's stored in an enclosed porch just off the kitchen, but there probably isn't any that's already split."

"I think I can manage," Mase said dryly.

While he was busy chopping wood out on the porch, Evie went to work in the kitchen, using the water she had heated on the stove to wash the dishes. She scrubbed out the sink and carefully polished the top of the range before she stepped out on the porch to join Mase, drawn by the muffled thunking sounds that came from the other side of the painted Dutch door.

It was almost as cold in the small, uninsulated enclosure as it was outside. The icy chill of the bare floor penetrated her warm socks within seconds and the cold made her toes curl.

Mase seemed unaware of the frigid temperature. A light sheen of perspiration covered his forehead from the exertion as he swung the axe repeatedly in steady, rhythmic strokes.

Reacting to the cold, and also to the sight of Mase's huge, muscular body, Evie felt her breasts tingle and grow taut. A deep flush colored her cheeks, and she was grateful for the dimness of the little room, which hid her reactions from his perceptive eyes.

"I'll start carrying some of this wood in," she said, anxious to provide herself with some practical reason for coming out.

She hurried to fill her arms with the rough logs, all too aware of the enigmatic eyes that followed her every movement. What emotions were hidden behind those deep, murky green orbs, she wondered warily? On second thought, perhaps she didn't want to know.

Mase watched Evie out of the corner of his eye, amazed to see the way she dug into the stack of wood he had just finished chopping. She piled the heavy logs one on top of the other in her arms with an expertise born of experience.

When she finished, the load she carried was almost as big as she was herself. None of the women he knew would have dreamed of taking on such a chore. They would have been afraid of breaking a nail or damaging their elegant, expensive clothes. Despite her petite frame, Mase sensed a wiry strength and determination that appealed to him.

He had never met a woman before who was so oblivious to her own attractions. She had puzzled him from the first, but the more he knew of her, the more the puzzle grew.

By the time she came out for her third load, Mase decided that they had enough wood to last the rest of the day. He set down his axe and started to load logs into his arms.

"Mase, you're bleeding," Evie exclaimed.

Mase looked down at his hand and saw the steady trickle of blood which had attracted her attention. It ran along the pad of his thumb, across his wrist, and down on to the wood.

"It's just a splinter," he replied, unconcerned. "I'll take care of it in a minute."

"Let me see it," she insisted, catching his hand and drawing it up toward the light.

"It's huge. Come into the house while I go find the first-aid kit. I'll take care of it for you," she insisted.

She returned a few minutes later, carrying a large, bright red metal case.

"Let's sit over on the window seat. The light's better there," she suggested, urging him toward it.

"You don't have to do this, Evie," he said,

reluctant to be in her debt for even that small favor. "I can take care of it myself."

"I don't mind," she assured him, searching through the kit for the items she needed.

Evie used a pair of tweezers to remove the splinter, being careful that it would not break off. A moment later, she disinfected the wound and smoothed a bandage over his hand.

"There you are," she said, her fingers lingering on the warm strength of that hand. "All done."

"You're a very good nurse," Mase said, his hand lying passive beneath hers. He felt strangely uneasy, not certain how he should respond to her kindness.

Evie sensed his hesitancy, and was touched by it. He was obviously unaccustomed to gentleness. All at once she felt protective, almost maternal toward him.

"When I was a little girl I wanted to be a nurse," she replied.

"Why did you change your mind?"

"Because as I got older I realized that I wasn't strong enough. I couldn't have stood watching the pain and suffering day after day."

"I think maybe you're stronger than you think you are, Evie," he said, his eyes caressing her with something akin to tenderness.

As they stared at each other the fire snapped loudly, and they jumped, moving apart.

"I . . . I'd better put this away," Evie stammered, clutching the first-aid kit to her breasts as she made a cowardly retreat up the stairs.

After lingering in the bedroom for as long as

she thought she dared, she went back to join Mase. When she entered the living room, she found him studying the contents of a shelf. He heard her enter and turned to her. His contemplative mood of a few minutes' past was gone.

"Feel like playing games?" he asked with a suggestive smile.

"What?"

"I found three games up here on the shelf. We've got our choice of chess, Monopoly, or Scrabble. That is, unless you'd rather spend the afternoon staring at the walls."

"Oh," she replied, relaxing slightly. "Sure, I'd like to play. How about Scrabble?"

Evie had never heard of anyone being seduced with a game of Scrabble before, but she had the strangest feeling that Mase was doing precisely that. They settled themselves on the carpet in front of the fireplace, drawing their allotment of letters. They were prepared to play.

The game started off innocently enough as Evie set out the word REFER. Mase countered with CUDDLE. Unsuspecting, Evie came back with CAT. Slowly, with deliberation, Mase put together the squares to form SPOON.

She cast him a suspicious glance. Somehow she did not think he had an eating utensil in mind. Evie persevered, adding five letters to form the word TEMPER, as if in warning. Mase ignored her less than subtle hint. The next word he added was CARESS. She was beginning to believe that Mase meant what he spelled.

Drumming her fingers on the soft carpet, Evie

studied the board before her. HIT, she added with a flourish.

CHEST. Against her will, her eyes rose to that broad, manly expanse, studying its slow, seductive rise and fall. He was far too good at this.

PURE.

"You can't use that, Evie," he said with a twinkle in his sexy green eyes.

"Why can't I?"

"Because that leaves two E's in a row, and EE isn't a word."

"I wasn't finished yet," she admonished, laying down an L to form EEL.

"Not bad," he said grudgingly.

PLEASURE. Mase leaned back, a self-satisfied look on his face. The ball was back in her court.

She settled for NO. Not too original, but it was the best she could do.

KISS.

Evie felt the emerald fire in his eyes as they rested upon her flushed face. She tried to resist, but the deep, seductive heat drew her as a moth was drawn to a flame. She looked up hesitantly and in an instant, she was caught.

Mase reached out to her with his large hand, his lean fingers still, silently beckoning. Her hand reached out to clasp his, and he urged her toward him, carrying that little hand to his lips and pressing hot, damp kisses into her palm. His tongue caressed the sensitive flesh, and she jerked back as though she had been scalded.

She sprang to her feet, ignoring the shaft of pain that the abrupt movement caused. Mase was just as quick. He caught her arm and held her close. Puzzlement at her sudden change in mood was evident on his face.

"Evie?"

"I'm tired of this game, Mase. Besides, my knee is hurting from sitting on the floor for so long. I'll see about some dinner."

Mase wasn't certain exactly what had happened. One moment everything was progressing according to plan, and the next . . .

With the skill of a practiced hunter, he backed off, allowing her to escape. Evie was very different from any woman he had known in the past. He would have to proceed with great care, or he would frighten her off completely. Suddenly, preventing that was the most important thing in the world.

In the solitude of the cold, dark kitchen, Evie tried to analyze her reaction. What was the matter with her tonight? They had just been playing a game. Why had it upset her so much?

Of course, she *had* been on edge all day. She had little faith in men's promises or good intentions. In her experience, promises meant little when a man wanted something.

Every man Evie had ever known, with the exception of her uncle, had wanted something from her. When she'd been reluctant to give it to them, they hadn't hesitated to try to take it, either with cunning or with outright force. She had spent a lifetime building up defenses against that kind of power play, but perhaps now she had begun to see such maneuvers where they did not exist.

Should she give Mase the benefit of the doubt? she asked herself hesitantly. After all, he had been a perfect gentleman so far, and Evie knew that she would have been in a lot of trouble if he hadn't stopped to help her out on the highway. He had really *earned* the benefit of that doubt.

Her problem was that she worried too much, she decided with a deep sigh. For the time being, she would accept Mase at face value. There would be time enough to worry when or if the problem came up.

Evie checked the cupboard and found nothing but soup, baked beans, two jars of sauerkraut, and a bag of marshmallows. It was not a promising dinner menu. She had never seen the kitchen so barren. Her aunt and uncle must have gone into town to do their shopping.

She crossed the half-dark room and opened the door of the refrigerator to peer in. Hmm, it was starting to feel warm in there.

She gathered up the meat and half-empty carton of eggs and set them out on the floor of the cold, enclosed porch. She eyed the two rib steaks longingly, but knew that she couldn't do them justice by cooking them on top of the stove. The hot dogs would be a better idea.

She gathered the condiments out of the tepid refrigerator, setting them out on the countertop. Then she opened the baked beans into a pan on the stove to heat.

Evie sensed Mase's presence long before she

turned to look behind her. She was not surprised to find him watching her from the doorway. He looked at her questioningly, as if he were trying to determine her mood.

Her smile was no more than a slight curving of the corners of her lips, but when Mase saw it, he relaxed, moving farther into the room.

"Did you find anything that looks good for dinner?" he asked.

"Well, that all depends. How does hot dogs and beans sound?"

"Sounds fine," he replied.

"That's good, because that's about all I could find. The beans are heating on the stove and I thought we could roast the hot dogs over the fire."

"Great. How about some wine to go with them?"

"Wine?" She wrinkled up her nose. "What kind of wine would go with hot dogs?"

"Rosé, I guess. It's supposed to go with anything."

The hot dogs sizzled on the long wooden sticks which her uncle kept ready in a cupboard, dripping fragrant juices on the embers of the fire. Mase and Evie stretched out comfortably on the floor, their backs propped up against the couch, relishing the steady heat of that fire. Plates holding bread and scoops of rapidly cooling beans waited on the floor beside them.

"You know, we've been talking all day, but I really don't know much about you," Mase said.

"What do you want to know?"

"For a start, what sort of 'responsibilities' are waiting for you back in town. A job or . . . ?"

"My business," she replied. "I own a small restaurant, Eva's Dinner Haus. It's only open in the evening, but we have beer and wine and live entertainment, so we usually manage to attract a good crowd. My cook is Austrian, and she makes the most delicious Bavarian-style meals you could imagine."

"Have you owned the restaurant long?"

"For almost three years."

"You must have been awfully young when you got started," he probed.

"Not really. I was twenty-three," she replied, puzzled by the look that crossed his face. It almost seemed to be one of satisfaction.

"It sounds like it means a lot to you," Mase observed. "I can understand why you're worried about it."

"I really don't have any reason to be," she confessed. "My employees know what they're doing, and, besides, with the weather as bad as it is, everything in town is probably closed up. That's enough about me, anyway. What about you? What kind of business are you in?"

"I'm on leave from the Army right now," he said.

"You mean on vacation?"

"In a way," he hedged.

"Where is your home?" she pressed.

"I'm stationed in California, but I don't really think of it as home."

"That sounds kind of lonely," she observed,

her eyes a bit sad. "Why don't you think of it as home?"

"Because it isn't," he returned with perverse logic.

His shuttered expression kept Evie from pressing him further. She didn't want him to think she was prying into his personal life. She had never known anyone quite like him. She was accustomed to life in a small town, where everyone knew all there was to know about everyone else.

"My home is too important to me. I couldn't live that way," she said softly. "I did when I was growing up. My stepfather was a wanderer. Until I came to live here with my aunt and uncle, I'd never even gotten to go through a whole year of school in the same town. I had no friends, no stability. No roots, I guess you'd say. The security of my life here means a lot to me."

Evie finished her wine, and Mase casually reached for the bottle to refill her glass. She pulled her hot dog out of the fireplace and studied it.

"I think they're about ready," she announced, reaching for her plate.

They ate in silence, bites of flavorful hot dogs and savory baked beans interspersed with sips of the heady wine. Evie was feeling pleasantly high by the time they finished their meal. She picked up the bag of marshmallows and dangled it temptingly between her thumb and forefinger as she looked up into his face.

"How about dessert?"

"Sounds good," he said with a smile. "I

haven't toasted marshmallows since I was a kid. I used to be pretty good at it.''

Mase and Evie speared the sweet white puffs on the ends of their sticks, carefully positioning them over the hot red coals. They watched them bubble and swell, waiting until they turned just the right shade of golden brown before pulling them back and easing them off their sticks.

"Umm, heaven," Evie said, a look of sheer bliss transforming her face as she popped the gooey ball into her mouth and licked her fingers clean.

"It's nice to know I haven't lost my touch," Mase said as he ate his own. His eyes fastened on her mouth as her tongue darted out provocatively to catch a sticky smear on her upper lip.

"You missed a spot," Mase said huskily, his finger catching the trace of white stickiness and carrying it to his own mouth.

Evie's lips trembled slightly as Mase caressed her mouth with his eyes. She watched, enthralled, as his lips descended toward hers. She could not find the breath to protest, and as the warmth of his mouth closed over her feminine softness, she lost all desire to do so.

The touch of his full, masculine lips on hers was incredibly pleasurable. He teased her with brief, tantalizing little kisses until she shifted against him, her arms winding around his neck to urge him closer.

Warm flesh melded to warm flesh, and when her mouth opened invitingly, Mase could not resist exploring each hidden recess she offered to him. He used his mouth with an expertise that took

Evie's breath away. She moaned softly and pressed herself more fully against his long body.

She did not understand her response to his kisses. Her breasts grew full and heavy as they rested on the hardness of his broad chest. After twenty-four hours of freezing, her whole body suddenly felt hot and flushed, as if she had a fever. That heat flowed through her, settling deep within her abdomen.

Mase's hands gripped the soft roundness of her bottom, pressing her hips tightly against his taut thighs. The heat of his manhood burned through the double layers of denim as if they didn't exist.

His tongue lured hers into his waiting mouth, sucking at it hungrily. Evie was overwhelmed by the pleasure of the sensation. She was hardly aware of it when he eased his grip on her and slipped his hand between their bodies to cup the roundness of a flannel-clad breast.

The rosy bud at its center blossomed and swelled against his palm, and encouraged, Mase rolled her over on her back. His powerful thigh slid between her slim ones, and all at once her muddled mind cleared.

Dear heaven, what was she doing? This man was a stranger to her, and she was nearly . . .

Hands that moments before had clung to him began to push feverishly against the hard expanse of his chest. His arms tightened around her instinctively, trying to hold her to him, to communicate his need to her, but a wave of sheer panic swept over her, and she began to fight him in earnest.

"No, please, Mase," she pleaded.

The fear in her voice finally reached him. As his grip on her loosened, Evie pulled herself out of his arms, scooting away from him.

Her fingers trembled and she curled up into a ball, hugging her knees against her heaving breasts. Her wide, stormy gray eyes displayed an odd combination of fear and unsatisfied passion.

Mase stared at her in surprise, not understanding the reason for her sudden withdrawal, but all too aware of her fear. He moved toward her, wanting to give comfort, but Evie shrank away from him.

His emerald-green eyes darted over to a nearby chair and the neatly folded blanket which rested there. Mase caught it in one large hand and tugged it toward him, unfolding the soft expanse of pale-blue wool and deftly flipping it around her small, huddled form. He sat beside her and pulled her firmly into his strong arms, tucking the blanket around her and hugging her as he would a frightened child.

She struggled at first, but he held her securely, rocking her until she let out a long, ragged breath and sagged against him.

"Oh, Mase, I'm so sorry," she quavered, her cheeks growing flushed as she realized what she had done.

"Hey, it's all right."

"No it's not," she denied. "I can't believe I did that. I've never had anything but contempt for women who tease."

"You're not a tease, Evie," he reassured her, and oddly enough, he believed it himself. There was no denying how frightened she had been just a few moments before. "We just got a little carried away. It was probably for the best that you called a halt to it. I know *I* was past the point of being able to do it."

"But why . . ." she started to question him, but stopped herself.

"Why what?"

"Why could *I* stop when *you* couldn't?" she asked, her face flushing beet-red. She dropped her eyes to the floor, unable to meet his knowing gaze.

Mase didn't know when he'd had more trouble answering a simple question. Evie had asked it with such naiveté that he just couldn't bring himself to answer her in the plain, clinical terms with which he was familiar.

The men in Evie's past must have been real winners if they hadn't even taught her that basic lesson about the male of the species, he thought derisively.

"Men are contrary characters at times, Evie," he answered at last. "When we're aroused, we tend to bypass our brains and think with another part of our anatomies. It's different for a woman.

"It . . . uh, looks like our wood supply is getting low again. I think I'll fill the wood box for the night. I won't be long."

He rose and started out of the room, but Evie's soft voice stopped him.

"Mase?"

"Hmm?" he inquired, turning to face her.

"You're a nice man."

THREE

Small lacy snowflakes continued to fall very heavily, as they had all day, adding to the thick white blanket that covered the earth. The howling wind had stopped sometime during the evening, and the eerie silence of the frozen world outside the warm lamplit house was complete.

Evie curled up comfortably in the soft armchair with her slim legs tucked up under her and her arms wrapped protectively around her waist. She stared into the glow of the crackling, undulating blaze without really seeing it.

Evie had been shocked by her encounter with Mase, not because of *his* actions, but because of her own. Had Mase been shocked, too? Evie didn't think so. Perhaps he was more accustomed to such things than she was.

A silent, humorless chuckle ran through her. That was a pretty safe assumption, Evie thought, feeling sorry for herself.

Her lack of experience had never troubled her before, but now, for some reason she couldn't explain even to herself, she wished she were more sophisticated. She had never felt this kind of attraction for any man; certainly not for her former fiancé, and she was forced to admit that she didn't have the slightest idea how to handle it.

"Look on the bright side," she told herself in frustration. "You probably don't have a thing to worry about. After that fiasco tonight, he probably wouldn't have anything to do with you again if you were the last woman on earth."

The thought left her even more depressed than she was before.

What had Mase meant when he'd said it was different for a woman? She couldn't believe the intensity of his need had been any greater than her own. She had never before experienced anything so overwhelming. Even in the beginning of their relationship, when Allen had touched her and kissed her, she had felt nothing. It had to be something else.

Perhaps an age-old instinct for self-preservation had made her draw back. The experience she had gained during the short months of her engagement had proved that women were far more vulnerable to hurt in such an encounter. At least it had proved it to her.

Mase's attitude had amazed her. She had expected him to be furious with her for leading him on, and she couldn't deny that she had done just that. It was not like her to give a man mixed signals. The fact that Mase had caused her to do so disturbed her greatly. She had thought she was one of those women who were unable to respond sexually to a man. Allen had told her that often enough. Now it appeared that she was wrong.

Evie glanced across the room to the huge picture window and stared out into the snowy night, allowing her mind to stray.

What would it be like to love and be loved by Mason Kincaid? To be contentedly waiting out the storm in their own home, secure and happy, with a lifetime of such nights stretched out before them?

It was the first time in four years that Evie had allowed herself such thoughts. She tried to tell herself that they were nonsense, but deep inside, a tiny voice persisted. Perhaps this could be the man who would make her forget the past.

Don't be stupid, she berated herself silently. From all Mase had said, and more importantly, what he *hadn't* said, he was very much like her irresponsible stepfather.

Both were big men, their shoulders broad and sturdy, but Kyle Richards's shoulders had borne the responsibility of a wife and stepdaughter badly. He was a drifter, always looking for a way to make easy money, never content to settle down and provide a secure life for his family. And to all appearances, Mase was just like him.

Thoroughly sick of the company of her own thoughts, she began to roam around the room, idly examining the contents of the bookshelves. Nothing there held her attention for long. Maybe a snack would help.

When she entered the kitchen, she was surprised to find Mase puttering around the big, dimly lit room. He was pouring steaming, fragrant liquid from a pan into two heavy earthenware mugs, working with the clumsiness of one unfamiliar with a kitchen. A bit of the liquid sloshed over the rim of a mug, and he paused to wipe it up with a well-used dish towel.

A tiny, affectionate smile turned up the corners of her mouth, and she sniffed appreciatively at the sweet, heavy scent of chocolate in the air.

"And you said you couldn't cook," she admonished, startling him so much that he nearly dropped the empty pan.

Mase glanced at her hesitantly. For a long moment he just stood there, mesmerized by the smile he found on her lips. Finally, an answering one started in his eyes and grew.

"I only heated milk and chocolate syrup in a pan," he corrected good-humoredly. "That doesn't exactly qualify me as a gourmet chef."

"Well, it sounds much better than any gourmet cooking I can think of right now. Thanks, Mase."

The double meaning behind her thanks was not lost on him. He winked encouragingly as he waved her back toward the living room.

"Let's go back in by the fire," he said, his smile turning mischievous. "I almost froze my tail off while I chopped the wood. I swear, if that pan of hot chocolate had been bigger, I'd have been tempted to climb in and take a bath."

"It *would* have warmed you up all right, but you'd have gotten awfully sticky," she commented.

"Don't tempt me to suggest the obvious solution to *that* problem," he retorted.

Without speaking, Evie turned and headed back to the other room.

He should have bitten his tongue off for that last crack, Mase berated himself. Her friendly companionship of moments before disappeared in front of his eyes, leaving her quiet and contemplative once again.

She settled back on the couch with studied casualness, leaving the comfortable armchair empty for Mase. He foiled her by settling himself next to her on the long corduroy couch and propping his feet up on the coffee table.

Evie tried to focus her eyes on the steaming mug, but against her will, they traveled along the long legs stretched out before her. She paused to admire the massive, hard-muscled thighs, remembering how they had felt when pressed tightly against her own legs and wondering how they would feel beneath the curious touch of her sensitive fingertips. His body had felt very good to her. Too good, in fact.

Mase shifted his position and Evie jumped, an embarrassed flush suffusing her cheeks. Instinctively, she shrunk back into the corner of the couch.

Mase misinterpreted her action and lost his temper.

"Damn it, Evie," he thundered. "You might think you'd never been alone with a man before. You're acting like a scared virgin. Would it make you feel any better if I told you I haven't raped a woman yet, and that I don't feel inclined to start tonight?''

It was the last straw. Embarrassment and the accumulated tension of the day caused tears to flood her eyes. She clasped her hands in her lap and stared down at them, unable to meet his angry gaze.

When Mase looked into her face, his anger dissipated and a strangely arrested expression gleamed in his smoky green eyes.

''My God,'' he said weakly. ''*Are* you a virgin?''

Under different circumstances, Evie might have smiled at the horrified expression on Mase's face, but this was one subject she could not connect with humor. Her eyes took on the icy silver color of the stormy winter sky.

''That isn't a subject I usually discuss with strangers,'' she responded, maintaining an outwardly cool appearance.

Mase flushed, as embarrassed as Evie by the question he had thoughtlessly blurted out.

''Sorry,'' he apologized. ''How about a truce? If I give you my word of honor not to make any more attempts on your virtue tonight, can we get some sleep?''

She studied him intently for a moment, her head tilted slightly to the side and a thoughtful expression on her face as if she was considering his proposal.

''That sounds fair enough,'' she said at last. ''But I'm going to hold you to it.''

"I always keep my promises, Evie," he replied. "Remember that."

Late into the night, Evie woke up shivering. The wind had come up again, and chilly gusts of air found their way under her blanket to nip at her bare feet and legs and up her body. The fire had died down to smoky, hissing coals as they slept.

Desperate for warmth, she crept closer to the hearth and added several of the smaller pieces of wood to the coals. She blew carefully on the fading embers, hoping for a spark to ignite the tinder.

Finally, she sat back on her heels, hugging her trembling, flannel-clad body as the fire snapped and began to curl around the wood. She was a bit sorry that she'd discarded her jeans to sleep in only her shirt.

"Evie?" Mase whispered from behind her. "Are you all right?"

"Yes," she returned. "I'm j-just so cold. I'm trying to build the fire back up."

"Come over here."

She rose questioningly to her knees and clambered across the old quilt to his side. Mase caught the corner of her blanket and drew it off her shoulders. He spread it atop his own, tucking it in behind him and lifting it in front of him in invitation.

"Come on, Evie," he said in a soft, persuasive voice. "Climb in with me. I'll warm you up."

"Mase . . . ?" she hesitated.

"It's okay, honey," he reassured her. "We can't stay up the whole night to keep building up the fire. All I'm suggesting is that we share a little body heat. Don't worry. I promise nothing will happen that you don't want.''

Evie hesitated a moment longer before surrendering with a sigh. When she slipped under the blankets, Mase's muscular arm caught her around the waist and tugged her tightly against him.

They fit together perfectly, with her back pressed up against his chest, her bare legs resting on top of his hard, muscular ones. His firm chin nestled comfortably on the gentle slope of her shoulder. She tensed as his hair-roughened forearm pressed lightly against the softness of her breasts. The feeling was incredibly intimate.

Soft, even breath whispered against her ear for long moments before she became aware of it. Mase was asleep.

Evie allowed herself to relax against the hard, masculine chest that supported her back, reveling in the protective arms that encircled her.

For the first time in a long while, she did not feel alone. It was nice to have someone to share the long, dark hours of the night with. It made her feel less afraid. His big body radiated heat which penetrated Evie to the marrow of her bones. Somehow she knew that the nightmare would not come that night.

FOUR

When Evie awoke, she was alone. The blankets had been considerately tucked in around her and the comforting warmth of the crackling fire encompassed her, but she missed Mase's presence beside her.

She buried her face in the pillow, trying to shut out the intruding light that shone in through the window. The warm, masculine smell of him lingered there in the feathery softness, tantalizing her sleepy senses, and she smiled a secret, very feminine smile.

She was so comfortable and lazily content within the warm cocoon of blankets that she wished the night could go on forever but dawn had broken, and it was already over. The cold gray light of morning beckoned to her, drawing Evie to the window.

She clutched the warmth of the heavy blanket around her as she stared out into the vast whiteness. The sky was still a solid, monotonous gray, but it was noticeably lighter than it had been the day before. The heavy fall of snow had slowed down to a few scattered flakes. Tiny gusts, remnants of the wind that had come up during the night, still whipped at the snow, stirring it into a semblance of its previous fury.

The wind had changed directions during the night, Evie realized with relief. It was no longer coming from the cold northeast where the storm had originated. That was the reason for the welcome change in the weather.

"Good morning," Mase said.

Evie whirled around to find him standing in the doorway. His shirtsleeves were rolled up to expose muscular forearms, and a dish towel apron was tucked into the waistband of his jeans, emphasizing his lean waist and narrow hips. He looked much too good for Evie's peace of mind.

"You'd better get moving, sleepyhead. I've been up for an hour and breakfast is almost ready."

A few minutes later they sat down to a meal of light, heavenly pancakes smothered in real butter and Vermont maple syrup. Evie didn't see how they could possibly taste as good as they smelled, but found that they did.

"I thought you said you couldn't cook," Evie chided with a smile. "These are wonderful."

"I guess I just don't think of pancakes as real cooking. I was raised by my grandfather. He loved pancakes and he taught me to make them when I was a kid."

Unfortunately, Mase's skill did not extend to making coffee. The dark, thick brew she poured into her cup reminded her of the black sludge they had drained out of her car at the gas station last week.

She creamed and sugared it heavily and plastered a smile on her face as she attempted to take a sip of it. Mase drank his black, seeming not to notice anything amiss. Obviously the man liked sludge.

"We'll be able to make it to town today," Evie observed optimistically. "It shouldn't take too long to dig your pickup out. With any luck, we'll make it by lunchtime."

"Will they have sanded the highway by then?"

"They probably have already."

"Well," he said, sopping up the last drop of syrup with the last bite of pancake, "let's get going then."

It took them nearly two hours to dig his battered old truck out of its snowy bed. When they finished, they went inside to straighten up the house and get warm again before setting out.

Evie glanced reluctantly around the living room as they were leaving. She was sorry to see their time together end. Would she ever see Mase again?

The trip down the driveway was slow and treacherous, but when they reached the main road, they found that it was freshly plowed and sanded. The remainder of the trip was accomplished with ease.

"I never did ask why you were conveniently driving by the other night," she said curiously. "I guess I was too grateful that you did to question my luck. Are you heading for Leavenworth or just passing through? We're a long way from California."

"I'm planning to stay for a while," Mase answered. "My grandfather lived in Seattle. He died recently, and I came home to settle things. While I was here, a friend offered to let me use his ski cabin near Leavenworth. It sounded like a good place to do some thinking."

"Is this your friend's pickup, too?"

"No, it's mine," he replied. "Why do you ask?"

"It's really none of my business," she said, embarrassed. "This pickup just isn't the kind of thing I pictured you driving."

"What *did* you picture me in, Evie? An expensive little sports car?" he asked with amusement. "I did try one out once. It took me a good five minutes to work myself in behind the wheel, and when I had, my knees were up by my ears. Those things just weren't made for people my size. Actually, this truck belonged to my grandfather. I couldn't bring myself to part with it. I learned to drive in this thing."

"It looks like we made it," Evie observed unnecessarily, her eyes discerning the slopes of the snow-covered roofs of Leavenworth, the quaint little Bavarian village which she had called home for the last fourteen years.

"You can just drop me here at the edge of town. There's no need for you to take me to my door."

RAINBOW WISHES / 59

"It's no trouble," he replied, his voice distantly polite. "Where do you live?"

"Over there," she answered, pointing to a two-story building with a sign proclaiming it to be Eva's Dinner Haus.

"Thanks for everything, Mase."

"Hey, don't sound so final," he said, a smile finally breaking the solemnity of his face. "You're not getting rid of me that easily. You'll be seeing me again."

Sure she would, she thought as she climbed out on to the slippery street. When pigs fly.

Her apartment was cold and empty when Evie let herself in. That was odd, she thought. Since they hadn't passed her aunt and uncle on the road, she'd expected to find them here. Besides, it wouldn't have gotten that cold in her apartment in an hour or two.

She put the questions aside for the time being, concentrating instead on running a scalding hot bath. She poured a generous dollop of her best bath oil under the tap and eased her tired, chilled body into the old porcelain tub, sliding down until she was submerged up to her neck in the hot, scented water. If she had been a cat, she would have been purring her pleasure.

It was more than an hour later when she finally emerged from the bathroom, wrapped in her favorite old fuzzy pink robe. She was already warm and sleepy when she curled up contentedly on her bed and called her cousin, Susan, for news of her aunt and uncle.

After a full half hour of being "entertained" with stories of the cute things Susan's little son Jeremy had done, Evie was smothering her third yawn in as many minutes. She excused herself and rang off.

It was just like her aunt and uncle to be safely visiting friends in the next town while she worried about them, she thought. She stretched lazily before drifting off to sleep.

Evie awoke to total darkness, confused and unsure of where she was. She lay there for a moment listening to the quiet until the familiar thud and hiss of the radiator assured her that she was at home.

What was Mase doing, she wondered? Would she see him again, as he had promised? She could see little reason why he would want to see *her*.

A man like Mase would be accustomed to worldly, sophisticated women. He had called her a scared virgin, Evie remembered, and in a way, he was right. That there were good reasons for her fear, she couldn't bring herself to explain to him. The dark secret from her past was something she had never told anyone, for even though it was part of *her* past, the secret was not hers to tell.

Evie shook off the thought, checking her alarm clock for the time. Good grief, it was almost six o'clock! She was due downstairs in a few minutes.

She splashed her face with cold water and patted it dry. Working quickly, she applied a discreet mauve eye shadow to emphasize the silver of her eyes, brushed pink blusher over her cheekbones, and finished with a coat of soft pink lip gloss.

Five minutes later she stood in front of the mirror, dressed in a gray wool skirt and soft, ice-blue angora sweater. With quick efficiency, she put the finishing touches on the simple knot of hair that rested on the nape of her neck.

Evie rushed down the stairs to the door which opened into her office, pausing to slip into her gray leather high-heeled shoes before walking out.

Evie was not surprised to find everything running smoothly. Her employees, Liesel and Ben, knew just as much about running the restaurant as she did. Luscious aromas wafted out of the kitchen into the dining room, reminding Evie that she hadn't eaten anything since early that morning. Her stomach growled inelegantly.

"Evie, dere you are, dear," Liesel's lilting, faintly accented voice greeted her. "I'm so glad you got back safely. I don't understand why you had to go after the supplies yourself. It vas lucky that you did not haf any trouble. Did you decide to stay over in Seattle?"

"No," she admitted reluctantly. "I *tried* to come home. Unfortunately, my car went off the road near my uncle's house and I wound up staying there for the past couple of days."

"Need some help getting the car home?" Ben asked.

"No thanks, Ben. I'll just call the service station tomorrow and have them tow it in."

"By the way," Liesel interjected. "Janie has the flu. We haf no one to entertain tonight."

"It's a shame that Janie's sick, but we'll manage. Until a year ago, I handled the entertainment every night. Did we have any problems from the storm?"

They made an attractive couple, Evie thought, pleased by the closeness that had grown between her two friends in the past three years. They were much the same height, Liesel being the taller by no more than an inch. Her slender, wiry frame was complemented by Ben's stocky build, which was still muscular, due to the physical activity that was a part of his daily life.

"Nope," Ben drawled. "Everything's fine here. You should've called me about your car though. We could have gotten it back here today."

"How did you get to your uncle's house, Evie?" Liesel continued her interrogation. "The storm vas so bad. You didn't try to walk, did you?"

"No," she replied. "Someone stopped and gave me a ride."

"Evie," Liesel said, scandalized. "You didn't just get into a car with a stranger, did you?"

"I didn't really have a lot of choice," she said, trying to control her irritation. "Would you rather I'd stayed where I was and frozen to death?"

Fortunately, a group of customers walked in before the older woman had time to formulate a reply. After that, the evening grew too busy for them to think about anything except their work.

Evie took her usual place beside the front door, where she greeted her customers and escorted them to their tables. Several village girls waited on the tables, while Liesel reigned supreme in the kitchen and Ben made himself useful in a countless variety of ways.

Between acting as hostess and handling the entertainment, Evie expected to be far too busy to think about anything or anyone. To her surprise, however, she found herself jumping nervously each time the door opened.

Too often throughout the evening, her eyes were drawn to the big front window. She had an uncomfortable feeling that someone outside was watching her.

It seemed as though the evening would never end, but finally it was time to close. The same uneasy feeling followed her upstairs into her apartment.

Perhaps she was just overtired. In the morning she would probably laugh over her silly night fears, but somehow she did not think she would.

FIVE

Evie's life soon fell back into its familiar routine, but by her third night back, the feeling of being watched continued to plague her. No one had approached her, but each time she stood before the windows in the front of the building, the uncomfortable sensation came over her. At times, she wondered if she were going crazy.

She had given up on seeing Mase again, and she had decided that it was probably for the best. There was no place in her life for the kind of involvement that would come from a relationship with him. She was happy with her life as it was, she tried to convince herself. Unfortunately, it wasn't working.

It had been a long, quiet night. Janie's bout with the flu had turned into a lengthy one, and Evie still found herself in charge of the entertainment.

It was almost a relief, she admitted to herself. At least when she spent the evening behind the big piano, those mysterious, watching eyes were not upon her. Evie loved music, and it was easy for her to lose herself in it, forgetting for a time the problems and disappointments of her everyday life.

A bell jingled as the front door opened, and a gust of frigid air burst over her. She glanced up to find Mase standing a few feet from her. Her fingers fumbled slightly over the keys, but she recovered quickly to complete the final chords of the song.

She hesitated for just a moment, trying to calm the nervous fluttering that suddenly filled her stomach. He had come back, but why? Evie rose to meet him.

"Hi," he greeted her with a smile. "I know I should have made a reservation, but do you think you could find me a table? Any little corner will do."

"I'll see what I can do. I have a little influence here. I know the management intimately."

"I only wish I could say the same," he replied, so softly that she wasn't sure she had heard him correctly.

After settling Mase at a table near the fireplace, she laid a menu before him and poured him a cup of coffee.

"You look lovely tonight, Evie," he said, his voice growing husky as he admired the swell of her breasts under the clinging sweater. "Can you join me?"

"Maybe for a few minutes," she agreed a bit reluctantly. "I've been playing the piano tonight, and I can't stop for too long."

"I know," he replied. "I've been listening to you. You play beautifully. What do you recommend for dinner?"

"The special tonight is very good. It's wiener schnitzel and potato dumplings."

"Hot dogs and dumplings?" he asked, staring at her with horrified fascination.

"No, Mase. Wiener schnitzel is veal," she explained, hiding a smile.

"Maybe I'll just have a steak," he hedged.

"Trust me. You'll like it," she promised. He did not look convinced. "What do you think of Leavenworth?"

"I haven't seen much of it so far," he replied. "I've been getting settled into my friend's cabin. I thought I'd check out the town tomorrow. If you're free, maybe we could have breakfast. I could pick you up around nine, if that's all right."

"I'd like that. I'll meet you here, though. I just live upstairs."

"Do you play the piano here every night?" he asked curiously. "You're very good."

"Thank you, but I'm just filling in for my regular entertainer while she's out with the flu. I love to play, though. I'd never played the piano until I came to live with my aunt and uncle. When they saw how much I liked music, my aunt Janet offered to give me lessons. I loved it right from the start. I'd practice for hours on end. My cousins thought I was crazy. They didn't understand what it meant to me. I'd never been allowed to do something just because I wanted to do it before."

Mase was puzzled by her words, but he saw the

sadness in her eyes, and his large hand reached out to cover hers. He was not experienced in giving comfort, and he didn't know what to say.

"Well . . ." she gave herself a little shake. "I'd better get back to work."

She stood and hurried back to the safety of her little corner. Mase stayed and watched her until late into the night.

Fortunately for Mase, the road to his cabin was relatively free of ice and snow and the traffic was nonexistent, for he was not concentrating on his driving. His thoughts were centered on a slender, dark-haired enchantress, as they had been since the night he'd met her.

Evie puzzled him, and Mase had a passion for puzzles that was rapidly being surpassed by his passion for her. How had any woman as warm and giving as Evie managed to avoid romance for so long? And more importantly, why had she wanted to do so?

The fires of her passion might be sleeping, but after the kisses they had shared that night during the storm, Mase had no doubt that they existed. They were just waiting for the right man to kindle them and send them bursting into flames. Like Sleeping Beauty, he thought whimsically. And he wanted to be the one who awakened her.

Was she still a virgin, he speculated? Even if she wasn't, he was convinced that she'd had little experience with men. Her response to him had been completely natural and lacking in the kind of guile he was accustomed to from women.

In the past he had always preferred his bed part-
ners to be experienced in giving and receiving
pleasure. He was a deeply sensual man, enjoying
the pleasures of sex but giving nothing of himself
in return, except for his body. The ideas of love
and commitment were foreign to him, and he
intended them to remain that way.

Painful memories from his childhood intruded
on the edges of his mind, but he forced them back.
He had heard that his parents had divorced several
years ago. His only reaction had been a fleeting
wish that they had done so thirty years earlier.

As a small child, Mase had been the innocent
victim of his parents' battles, and he had decided
long ago that he would never commit himself to
that kind of relationship. Sex was all he had ever
wanted from a woman, and it was all he wanted
from Evie. But if that were so, why hadn't he
pressed the issue while they were snowbound?

A troubled frown furrowed his brow, and he
shifted uncomfortably on the hard seat. If sex was
truly all he wanted, then why was he rapidly
becoming obsessed with the thought of being the
only man to know the passion that simmered
beneath her surface calm?

If he'd had any sense at all, he wouldn't have
gone to see her. He hadn't intended to when he
had driven into town for dinner, but the urge to
see her again had been almost irresistible.

It was just that she was a novelty to him, he
told himself at length. He had never come in close
contact with a woman like Evie before. Soon the

novelty would pall. He had lived this way for thirty-four years, and he was too old to change now.

The next day dawned clear and cold and bright. The sun shone down from a cloudless, intensely blue sky, reflecting off the broad expanse of whiteness and imbuing the snow with the radiance of finely cut crystal.

Mase's breath misted heavily in the fresh, icy air as he crossed the few steps from his pickup to the door of the restaurant where Evie awaited him. When he rapped on the door, the soft leather of his gloves muffled the sound, but just as he was about to knock again, the door swung open and she appeared before him.

"Hi," she greeted him with a breathless sound in her voice that could not be attributed to the cold.

"Hi," he returned. "Where would you like to go for breakfast?"

"There's a good place up at the end of the street."

"Okay, let's try it."

The small cafe was obviously a popular local spot. It was bustling with activity, and they had to wait in line to be seated at their table, which was near the fireplace. They knew a moment of awkwardness, and they were thankful when the hostess, dressed in a Bavarian peasant costume, came to bring them coffee and menus.

Mase watched with amazement as Evie emptied half the pitcher of cream into her coffee. She caught the look and smiled ruefully.

"I do like a *little* coffee with my cream. Actually, I don't like coffee very much. I have to drown the taste to get it down. Does anything sound good to you?" she went on. "I'm going to have a German pancake and sausages."

"What's a German pancake? Is it topped with sauerkraut or something?" he asked suspiciously.

"It's a pancake batter made with lots of cream and eggs and baked in the oven."

"It sounds interesting," he conceded. "I guess I'll try it."

Half an hour later, fortified by a substantial breakfast, they set out for Mase's tour of the town. To Evie's biased eyes, Leavenworth was always beautiful, but the picture perfect weather could only enhance its attractiveness.

The buildings all along the main street were decorated by murals on stuccoed walls. Old-world carvings around the doorways added to the decor, as did the hundreds of colored lights that trimmed every building, tree, and shrub.

"Just wait until dusk, when the lights come on," Evie said, justifiably proud of her village. "You've never seen anything as beautiful in your life."

As he took in her delicately flushed features Mase *could* think of something more beautiful, but he prudently kept silent. He didn't want to spoil the easy camaraderie that had marked their morning thus far.

The street was not long, but it still took them several hours to fully explore the many shops.

"I can't believe how many different kinds of

stores there are here," Mase commented as they entered a shop which sold nothing but cut crystal.

The shelves were filled with an amazing variety of merchandise, from elegant bowls and vases to tiny figurines of bears and clowns. The bright sunlight filtered into the room, casting rainbow reflections on to the ceiling, walls, and floor.

Mase was fascinated with a prism that sat in the front window, admiring the myriad of colors trapped within it.

"It's beautiful, isn't it?" Evie remarked, coming up behind him. "For my birthday one year, my aunt and uncle gave me a crystal drop to hang in my window. They called it a rainbow maker. I'd been looking at it for months. When I was little, my real father told me that if I made a wish as I looked at a rainbow, it would come true."

"I've never been much of a believer in wishing," he said pensively. "You can't just sit back and wait for things to happen. You have to go out and *make* them happen."

He reached out and picked up the prism. Colors danced across his fingers as if they were live things, and Mase was mesmerized by their movements.

"I'll take this," he told the waiting clerk, handing her what Evie considered an outrageous amount of money in exchange for the trinket. Mase never blinked an eye. He casually stuffed his purchase into his coat pocket.

Mase glanced up to find Evie staring raptly at a small crystal castle atop a silver-plated box. It was obviously the showpiece of the shop, and when she gazed at it, her eyes shone like a child staring into a toy store window.

"Would you like to hear it, Evie?" asked the woman behind the counter.

"Yes, please, Darla."

"It's beautiful," Mase murmured over the tinkling tones of the music box, thinking that it suited the woman before him.

A short time later, they stepped out into the cold once again. The sun was riding high in the sky and the brilliance was almost blinding.

"You know, that's the first souvenir I've ever bought," he said as they strolled along the street.

"But, Mase . . ." Evie protested. "In the Army you must have seen so many exciting places. Why haven't you—"

"They didn't mean anything to me," he interrupted. "Why would I want something to remember them by?"

She absorbed the implication of his words in silence. All of the exotic places he had seen meant nothing to him. Why was Leavenworth different? Her intuition told her that Mase was as puzzled by this as she was. He was a complicated man. Would she ever truly understand him?

"Are you hungry?" Mase asked, glancing at his watch. "It's after noon already."

"Not really," she replied. "I'm still full from breakfast. I don't usually eat that much. I should really get back to work, anyway."

Her attempt to bring their day together to an end was anything but subtle, but Mase was not prepared to give up that easily. He turned casually and followed her, just as if she had invited him along.

She glanced at him uncertainly. Obviously subtlety did not work with this man. Evie couldn't bring herself to be rude, so she guessed she would just have to make the best of it.

"Let's go around to the back door," she suggested reluctantly. "These locks are so much trouble that I hate to mess with them when I don't have to."

Even though the restaurant did not open for business for another five hours, the kitchen was already alive with the luscious aroma of the night's dinner special. People bustled about in an organized fashion that impressed Mase.

"Liesel," Evie called as she took off her hat and unwound the scarf from around her neck.

"Back here, Evie," called a feminine, softly accented voice in return.

"Come back with me for a moment, Mase," she invited. "I'd like to have you meet my cook, who also happens to be my very good friend."

They found Liesel bending over a huge stove, stirring a pot of sauce that was the source of the heavenly fragrance. When they approached, Liesel seemed surprised to see a man trailing after Evie, and she eyed him speculatively.

"Liesel, I'd like you to meet Mase Kincaid. Mase, this is the lady whose cooking you enjoyed so much last night."

"The genius, you mean," he corrected, turning

a smile on the older woman that could have charmed the birds out of the trees.

Liesel was no less susceptible than those birds, Evie noted, equal parts of humor and irritation warring for supremacy. She thought her cook had too much common sense to be taken in by a smile.

"You are too kind," she replied to the compliment, smiling appreciatively at the handsome couple he and her young employer made.

"Did you haf a good time today?"

"Yes, it was very nice," Mase replied for both of them. "You have a beautiful town. I can see why everyone is so proud of it.

"Well, I'd better be going for now. I can see that you're busy," he went on, turning to Evie. "Thanks for the tour. I really enjoyed today . . . so much that I was hoping you could have dinner with me tomorrow night."

"I'm sorry, Mase. I'd like to, but the restaurant keeps me pretty busy at night—"

"But, Evie . . ." Liesel interrupted unscrupulously. "Haf you forgotten that we are closed tomorrow night?"

"Oh." Evie hesitated, flashing Liesel a look that promised retribution.

Mase recognized an ally when he saw one, and he promptly began to play off her lead.

"Oh no, Liesel," he said with suspicious humility. "I wouldn't want Evie to feel like she was being forced to go out with me."

"I don't feel like I'm being forced," Evie denied halfheartedly. Her eyes met two pairs with similar expressions of wounded innocence.

The angelic expression on Mase's face proved to be her undoing. She burst into laughter.

"Thank you, Mase," she said at last. "I would be delighted to have dinner with you, but I have a feeling I've just been suckered."

SIX

The evening went much more smoothly than Evie had anticipated. As they dined on trout almondine at a local seafood restaurant, Mase set the pace of the conversation, talking comfortably on a number of innocuous subjects that were designed to set her at her ease.

At least he had the good sense not to gloat over her capitulation, Evie thought. She had been watching him closely all through dinner, and he was either a very good actor or he was really as innocent as he seemed. She did not think the latter prospect was likely.

It was still fairly early when they arrived back at her apartment. After fumbling for a moment to find her key, she turned to Mase and started to invite him inside.

His face was mere inches from hers, and his green eyes stared deeply into her silvery ones. Their breath mingled in a cloud of frosty mist. When his large hand cupped the side of her face, Evie opened her mouth to speak.

"Shh," Mase hushed her, laying his finger across her lips. "It's all right. I'm only going to kiss you, okay?"

She stood transfixed as his warm, moist lips closed slowly over hers. The feel of them rubbing back and forth across her slightly parted mouth was even more pleasurable than she remembered.

When his tongue urged her lips apart, all thought of resistance fled. Mase drew her more fully against him, encircling her with his strong arms. Evie sighed, her arms clutching involuntarily at his shoulders.

She slumped against him, conscious only of the taste of his mouth and the smell and feel of his big body. She wanted to lose herself in his strength, and the thought disturbed her.

After a time, Mase drew back. He soothed her passion-swollen lips with tiny, tender kisses, allowing her to come slowly back to earth before his supportive arms released her.

"Will you go out with me tomorrow night?" he invited.

"Yes, please," she replied dreamily.

"I'll see you at seven then," he said, reluctant to go.

His lips sought hers in one last searing kiss before he turned and walked away down the stairs. If he stayed a moment longer, Mase knew he would never have left.

The nightmare had come again last night. Evie had awakened in a cold sweat, shivering violently with a combination of fright and cold. Strange how that inexplicable cold always came in the aftermath of the nightmare.

After that, sleep was long in coming. When morning finally dawned, Evie dressed and made a large pot of coffee.

She was determined not to dwell on the coming night. She dragged her neglected account books out onto her desk and tried to concentrate on what was usually one of her favorite jobs.

After staring at the same page for a solid hour, she pushed the book aside in frustration. She went to the closet and pulled on her heavy coat. Perhaps fresh air and some company other than her own would help.

She soon discovered that browsing through the same shops she had visited with Mase two days before did not help at all. She couldn't get him out of her mind.

What made Mase so different? Why did she respond to him in a way she'd never before responded to any man?

And why in the world had she said she would go out with him again tonight? Only pride kept her from backing out on their date, she told herself. But was it really pride and nothing more? Honest to a fault, she was forced to admit that she wanted to see him again.

It had taken her a long time to overcome her fear of men after she came to live in Leavenworth. Uncle Jock had worked very hard to win her trust, and had finally achieved it. She had slowly come to believe that all men were not like her stepfather.

It had not been easy for her to leave her home

here in Leavenworth and venture out into the world. Although she had only gone to college in Seattle, Evie had been very lonely. In fact, she decided later, she had been easy prey for a man like Allen Pritchard.

He had been a regular customer in the small restaurant near the campus where she worked. He had always been friendly and easy to talk to, and once he had helped her out when another patron had tried to get a bit too friendly.

He had been attractive and charming, in a quiet, reserved sort of way. Like Evie, he had not had many friends. She had seen him as a kindred spirit, just as he had intended that she should. She soon discovered that the smiling, amiable man she had been attracted to only existed in her imagination.

After that one disastrous attempt at romance, Evie had decided that she could not trust her own judgment when it came to men. She had been determined never to allow any man to get that close to her again, and she had kept that promise until she met Mase.

She thought ahead to the coming night and wondered what would happen. Or perhaps she should be asking herself what she *wanted* to happen.

Evie fumbled through her purse for her key as Mase stood quietly behind her. The evening had been a repeat of the night before, she thought. At least so far. Her fingers closed around the errant key chain, trembling slightly as she opened the door.

"Would you like to come in for a brandy?" she asked tremulously, half hoping and half fearing that he would accept.

"Yes, I'd like that."

Evie turned on the lights and took off her coat. The black wool slacks and the bulky red knit sweater that she was wearing were hardly suggestive, but she felt somehow underdressed.

"It's chilly in here, isn't it?"

"Would you like me to start a fire?" Mase offered. "It looks like you've already got your fireplace set up for it."

"That sounds lovely. Excuse me for a moment and I'll get the brandy."

Mase looked around, absorbing the atmosphere of her small, homey apartment. The high, arched ceiling was very attractive with its bare, rustic-looking beams. Glossy hardwood floors were covered with worn Oriental rugs in soft, muted shades. The high walls were painted a warm shade of beige and adorned with several attractive landscapes by local artists. The style of her odd assortment of furniture could only be called Early Salvation Army.

Once the fire crackled in the plain brick fireplace, he went into her tiny bathroom to wash. Her influence could be felt there, too, in the ruffled lavender shower curtain and assorted female paraphernalia. When he passed back through her bedroom, he could not help but notice that the same ruffled, utterly feminine look pervaded that room also.

The dresser was very tidy, but numerous snapshots were attached to the mirror, and on the floor, forgotten in a corner, lay a pair of discarded panties and a lacy bra. Mase flushed guiltily, feeling like a voyeur.

When he rejoined her, they curled up comfortably on the floor. The brandy relaxed them, and they kicked off their shoes, moving closer together.

Evie's long hair was pinned into its usual coil at the nape of her neck, and Mase reached behind her and pulled out the pins. Dark, heavy tresses tumbled down around her shoulders in delightful disarray.

"I've been wanting to do that since the first time I saw you. You have beautiful hair. It's a crime to hide it the way you do."

"I don't hide it. It's just easier."

Mase inched closer, his fingers threading through the long, tangled curls. He carried one curl to his face and inhaled, relishing the soft, flowery fragrance.

"Would you like another brandy?" she asked.

"I don't need another drink." His husky voice came from very close to her ear. "I'm already drunk on the smell of you."

Evie jumped nervously as his arm came around her shoulders and drew her toward him. Her hand pressed lightly against his broad chest, as if in protest. His other arm crept stealthily around her, enclosing her so snugly that she scarcely had the breath to object.

When Mase's mouth closed over hers, she sighed and collapsed against him, her arms creeping around his neck to pull him closer.

Long moments passed as their tongues entered into a seductive mating dance. Lips caressed sweetly, and a soft sigh passed between them, neither his nor hers, but theirs.

His arms deserted her for a moment, but his mouth did not. His rough wool shirt, one of two barriers between them, went flying into a corner, unheeded and unmissed. His hands found the hem of her sweater and began to inch it up and over her head.

When his deft fingers moved to the fastening of her bra, Evie came back to earth in a rush.

"No, Mase, please don't."

"It's all right, honey," he said. "Trust me. I just want to see you, to touch you. I promise I won't try to make love to you."

His words soothed her and she allowed him to coax her back to his side. His fingers did their work and her bra went limp and was gone. With infinite gentleness, he eased her down onto her back. For a moment he simply looked at her, hungry for the sight of her bare flesh.

"You're so beautiful," he breathed.

His fingertips ran reverently across her soft, silken skin, and Evie quivered in response. His large hand cupped a round breast, gently molding and massaging the fragile heaviness.

Her nipple puckered, and Mase drew it into the hot silk of his mouth, his tongue teasing and tickling the throbbing bud until Evie gasped and moved beneath him. One hand went lower, unzipping her slacks and moving to the tiny triangle of curls which housed the center of his desire. Her hand caught frantically at his.

"No, please Mase," she pleaded. "You promised."

The marauding hand retreated at once. His arms cradled her against his chest and stroked up and down the slender column of her spine.

"It's all right, honey," he said. "See? I told you I always keep my promises."

He caught at the edge of the big afghan on the sofa and dragged it down to cover them. Lying peacefully in each other's arms, they fell asleep.

Evie awoke just before dawn to find herself once again snuggled spoon-style against Mase's hard body. Her back was pressed against his fur-covered chest, her hips were resting intimately in the cradle of his thighs. A muscular forearm encircled her waist, and one hand cupped the fullness of a bare breast.

Embarrassment flooded through her as she took in the intimacy of their positions. She tried to escape without awakening Mase, but when she shifted her position, he stirred.

Lean fingers gently massaged the soft breast they held captive. Evie shivered slightly, looking back over her shoulder to find Mase studying her with hot, smoldering eyes.

He brushed the dark curls off her shoulder and pressed warm, damp kisses in their place. A lean finger fanned over the sensitive peak, and Evie's back arched.

This time when his hand moved to unfasten her

slacks and burrow under her panties, seeking the softness of her woman's flesh, she did not demur.

He stroked and caressed her with infinite patience, his hard fingers worshipping her, teasing and stroking until she writhed against him.

The sensual tension built within Evie's body, frightening her with its intensity. She had not imagined such sensations existed. She clutched desperately at the hard, muscular arm that encircled her quivering torso. She needed something to cling to, and it was the only part of his body within her grasp.

As she approached the precipice, her breath came in labored pants. At last she slipped over the edge. Mase held her securely until the tremors which wracked her body ceased. Then he pressed soft kisses against her neck and shoulders.

For long moments, Evie lay against him, too utterly spent to move. She was aware only of the haven of security she found in his arms, and she wondered at the intensity of the pleasure he had given her.

. But the pleasure had been hers alone. Mase had given with no thought of himself, but Evie could feel his need in the tenseness of the muscles she clasped and the hard heat at the juncture of his thighs.

"Mase?" she hesitated.

"Hmm?"

"Do you . . . do you want to make love to me?"

He could feel her blush, even though he couldn't

see it. He was touched by her offer, but it was obvious that she wasn't ready for that final step.

"No, honey," he said tenderly, his fingers turning her chin so that their eyes met. "When we make love, it will be because you want me as much as I want you, not because you feel obligated to let me."

He quieted her halfhearted protest with a gentle caress of his lips. Drawing the covers over them, he held her until she slept.

SEVEN

When Evie awoke again, Mase was gone. She was relieved that she did not have to face him right away. This morning marked a milestone in her life. It would take some time to adjust to the change that had taken place.

She could no longer tell herself that she was not interested in sex. Evie tried to feel embarrassed by her abandoned behavior in Mase's arms last night, but couldn't. It had felt too right. It had never been anything like that with Allen.

She tried to remember how she had felt when Allen kissed her. All she could remember was awkwardness and a vague feeling of embarrassment.

Not just any man could inspire the need and hunger Mase had. He had been so unselfish, so giving. It would have taken very little effort on his part to make her give in completely. Hadn't she offered herself to him?

But Mase had been too proud to settle for that. That is, if he still wanted her.

Perhaps in her inexperience, she had done

something that repulsed him. Was that why he had left while she was sleeping?

Evie arose and went in to shower, feeling a bit sore and stiff. She was disturbed by her thoughts, and dressed quickly before going downstairs. She felt a need for some company other than her own.

She found the kitchen cold and dark and empty. Her shoulders slumped in disappointment. She had forgotten that they were closed today.

Still, it would be better to be busy, she decided. The large cookbook on the drain board caught her eye. She would bake a batch of Christmas cookies.

A few minutes later, all of the necessary ingredients stood side by side on the counter. Mixing bowls, sugar, flour, eggs, butter, and fragrant vanilla. All she needed was the sifter.

Why in the world had she hired a cook who stood a full six inches taller than herself, she wondered in frustration? The seldom-used sifter, she had discovered, sat on the highest shelf in the kitchen. Even with the aid of the stepstool, Evie could not reach it.

She was standing on that stool when a knock on the back door nearly startled her into falling. When she glanced in that direction, she saw Mase's face through the window.

Evie clambered down to the floor, struggling for composure. What was she going to say? She glanced at her reflection in the window and moaned silently. Her hair was a mess.

Just be calm, she told herself. She forced a smile to her lips as she opened the door.

"Hi," she said, eyeing him anxiously from under her lashes.

"Hi," he returned, taking in her flushed face and lowered eyes. "Need some help?"

"I was just trying to get the sifter down, but this darn stool isn't high enough."

"Let me try," Mase offered, walking over to the cupboard. He reached up and lifted the sifter down for her without the aid of the stool.

After setting it on the counter, he faced her, debating with himself over his next course of action. When their eyes met, his were filled with uncertainty, and Evie was touched.

She walked straight into his waiting arms. She hugged him tightly, burying her face in his coat, feeling safe and protected as she had during the long hours of the night. Mase raised her face up to his, and when his mouth sought hers, she yielded it eagerly.

The tension drained slowly from her body as they clung to each other. His large frame blocked out her doubts, and a new, exciting awareness took their place.

Long moments passed before Mase drew back. His arms still held her and his hand massaged her back.

"I really didn't mean to do that," he said. "I just stopped by to find out if you still want to go out with me tonight."

"Oh," she replied, puzzled. "I . . . Sure. If *you* still do."

"Of course *I* want to. I just thought you might have changed your mind."

Evie realized at last that Mase was feeling uneasy and a bit wary of her reaction to his love-making. He had always seemed so self-confident. This glimpse of vulnerability made her feel even closer to him.

"Why didn't you stay with me, Mase?"

"I thought it might make you uncomfortable. I didn't want to push you."

"Oh. Then it wasn't something I did? I was afraid I'd done something that had turned you off."

He stared at her for a moment, too astonished to speak. Finally he found his voice. "Honey, if I were any more turned *on*, you'd find yourself flat on your back on that table over there," he said.

Unconsciously, her gaze dropped below his belt. Faced with the evidence of his desire, her cheeks turned crimson and she looked away. His chuckle was low and sensual as he grasped her chin and turned her face up to his.

"I've never seen a woman blush like you do. You're adorable."

When their lips met again, their kiss was long and slow, like that of lovers of long standing. When he released her, she was reluctant to let him go.

"Are you in the middle of something that can't wait?" he asked.

"No. I was just going to bake some cookies."

"Then why wait until tonight? Let's go on a picnic."

"A picnic?" she responded incredulously.

"Mase, it's freezing outside. Maybe you haven't noticed, but the ground is covered with snow."

"I noticed," he quipped. "It's also a beautiful day. The sky is clear and the sun is out. It's a perfect day to go snowmobiling. We can stop down at the deli and get a couple of sandwiches. What do you say?"

Mase's enthusiasm was contagious. The dark quietness of the kitchen seemed less inviting by the minute.

"Why not?" she laughed impulsively.

Her ambivalent mood of moments before vanished under the warmth of Mase's smile. Suddenly the day seemed very bright and filled with excitement.

EIGHT

When they walked down the sidewalk toward the edge of town, it seemed to Evie that the main street was filled with far more people than usual. Many curious eyes followed their progress, and she knew their possible relationship was the source of much speculation.

With an uncharacteristic show of defiance, she slipped her hand through Mase's arm. She felt him hug it against his side. Even through his heavy jacket, she could feel the rock solid strength of that arm, and a tiny shiver worked its way down her spine. She remembered clearly the feel of that arm encircling her bare torso last night.

Evie was nervous of driving a snowmobile by herself the first time out, so when they left the small shop that provided ski and snowmobile rentals, she was riding along behind Mase. At first she wrapped her arms tightly around his lean waist and held on for dear life, out of nervousness.

But the clear, sunny day beckoned, and soon her fear dissipated. She lost herself to the pure exuberance of whooshing across the sparkling, crystalline snow. The motor thrummed and vibrated with energy beneath them, and she found herself hugging him, simply for the pleasure of feeling his big, hard body against hers.

Even while the sun shone warmly on their backs, the icy wind whipped across the snowy terrain to sting their faces. The machine seemed to fly across the pristine landscape, and she laughed aloud with delight at the sensation.

They were miles from town by the time Mase cut their speed and eased them to a stop. The noise and distraction of the highway seemed very far away. A stand of trees and the inevitable, encroaching shrubs that surrounded them, gave them more privacy than seemed possible out in the middle of a field.

"Ready for lunch?" he asked over his shoulder.

"I'm starving," she admitted, her breath a misty cloud in the stillness of the air.

"I hope their food is better than the advertising suggests," he said, making joking reference to the sign in the deli's window boasting *the wurst sandwiches in town.*"

"They wouldn't have stayed in business long if they weren't," Evie pointed out.

"I don't know," he pretended to ponder. "Maybe they depend on innocent tourists like me to support them."

"Mase, something tells me you weren't innocent even on the day you were born," she retorted.

A laugh rumbled deep within his chest, and his powerful shoulders shifted in a negligent shrug.

"You could be right," he said, his eyes gleaming.

Mase stamped down an area of the snowy ground to give them a spot to spread their blanket. Evie squatted on the bright red and blue plaid square, setting out thick pastrami sandwiches with dill pickles and potato salad, and pouring steaming cups of fragrant, orange spice tea from the thermos she had packed.

They stretched out side by side on the blanket. Mase's long, muscular legs almost brushed against her shorter, slender ones, and she resisted the temptation to shift restlessly beside him.

They ate leisurely, but without speaking. The only sound that penetrated the air was the soft rustling of the wind through the trees.

When they finished Mase laid down on the prickly wool of the blanket, settling his head, uninvited, on Evie's lap. She started in surprise, her body tensing slightly, but when he did nothing but lie there and close his eyes, she allowed herself to relax.

She leaned back, resting the gloved palms of her hands behind her on the blanket to support her body. The sun was warming her through her heavy layers of clothing and she was filled with a languid sensation of well-being.

"What's that building over there?" Mase asked, squinting as the sun reflected brightly on the snow.

Evie straightened and lifted a hand to shield her

eyes from the glare as she followed his pointing finger.

"That used to be a ski lodge," she explained, growing slightly breathless as his cheek rubbed absently back and forth across her thigh. "It was built about ten years ago, but there wasn't enough business to keep it open."

He shifted his body, and she gasped as his hand slid between her denim clad thighs, drawing teasing patterns across the sun warmed fabric.

"Mase, cut that out," she tried to command, but her voice trembled slightly.

His hard fingers moved tormentingly over the apex of those shapely limbs, and her breath caught in her throat. She clutched his brawny wrist with both of her hands and tried to move it, but she discovered that she couldn't budge him.

Changing her strategy, she started to scoot away from him, but he caged her legs between his thighs and held her still. A shiver that was not fear, but something else altogether, rippled through her.

She wiggled furiously under him for a long moment, before she realized her error in tactics. His body grew hot and hard against her leg. Knowledge flooded through her and she froze.

Mase paused, feeling the tension in her body. He inched up beside her until they were face to face. His hand brushed her cheek and he smiled ruefully down at her.

"I see you're getting to know *my* body, too. You're right. I want you, honey. But that doesn't mean I can't control my desire."

Her mind raced back to the previous night. He

had wanted her then, too, she remembered, but he had never lost control. Some of the tension left her.

"Feeling your body under mine this way is the most exquisite torture I've ever imagined. You'd think I would want it to stop, wouldn't you? But I don't. I want the teasing to go on forever."

His lips came down toward hers. His tongue outlined their delicate pinkness, and she shifted restlessly under him, but he did not kiss her.

"Who are you teasing?" she asked huskily. "Yourself, or me?"

"Maybe both of us," he admitted.

Her arms encircled his neck, urging him down until their mouths met at last. She flowered beneath him, and responding to her unspoken invitation, his tongue slid into the silken warmth behind her lips. He nudged her legs apart and made a place for himself between them.

A heightened urgency flowed through her. She was alive to the need within him, and a new, burgeoning need began within her, too. When he pulled back, she made a small, unintelligible sound of protest.

He rolled onto his side and carried her with him, hugging her tightly against his chest. The breath was hard and ragged in his throat as he forced his desire back.

"Mase . . ." she began tentatively.

"No, honey," he said, his fingers resting against her tender lips, hushing her. "The first time I make love to you is *not* going to be in a cold, snowy field. I'd probably get frostbite of the gluteus maximus. It would be too much for my sense of dignity to bear.''

"You're crazy, do you know that?'' she laughed softly, hiding her face against his shoulder.

"There have been times when I suspected it,'' he smiled, his voice nearly back to normal. "But when I'm around you, I'm *sure* of it.''

He bounded to his feet, ruthlessly pulling Evie up with him. She grumbled under her breath at his rough and ready methods, and he swatted her playfully on the rear.

"Come on, woman,'' he prodded, bending to gather up the remains of their picnic lunch. "Let's get moving. If we hang around here much longer, who knows what kind of trouble you'll get us into.''

"*I'll* get us into,'' she squeaked indignantly. "Who started it in the first place?''

She neither expected nor received an answer. While she packed up the picnic basket, Mase shook out the blanket and folded it neatly into a small bundle which fit into the storage compartment of their vehicle. A few minutes later, they were back on the snowmobile.

Deftly skirting a cluster of trees, Mase cut a path toward the distant outline of the old ski lodge. The smooth-moving machine beneath them glided across the ground. He dodged carefully around some boulders that were so evenly spaced that they had to have been set there for a purpose, coming to a halt before the huge double doors.

"It looks pretty overgrown,'' he observed.

"No one's been around here for a long time.

They kept a security guard for a while, but when they couldn't sell it, I guess they decided it wasn't worth the expense any longer."

"Let's take a closer look," he suggested, climbing off the low seat.

The long exposure to the cold was causing Evie's knee to stiffen up. When he noticed how she struggled to rise, Mase reached down and half lifted her to her feet.

"Are you all right, honey?" he asked with concern.

"I'm fine," she said emphatically. "I guess I'm just getting a little cold."

"I just want to take a quick look. Then we'll head back to town," he promised.

It really is a beautiful building, Evie thought to herself. In keeping with Leavenworth's theme, it looked like something straight out of the Bavarian alps.

"It was a shame about this place," she said, walking a bit stiffly behind Mase. "The town had just started to establish itself with the tourist trade when it was built. If it were open today, it would probably do a great business."

"Why do you think it would succeed now?" he asked curiously.

"Because the people who have come here for the festivals found out how beautiful the countryside is, and now they come year round. In the summer for fishing and hiking, and in the winter for cross-country skiing."

"I'm surprised no one has tried to re-open it."

"A few people have considered it," she told

him. "I guess they just thought it would take more time and money than they wanted to spend to get it into shape again. Seeing it close up, I can understand why."

Mase wiped his glove across a dust encrusted window pane and peered inside. Evie followed suit, and was surprised to find that the inside seemed fairly intact. Even some of the furnishings were still there.

She moved away and leaned against the side of the building, trying unobtrusively to rub her knee. The dull ache was steadily increasing in intensity.

Noticing the almost furtive movement, Mase turned and watched her. A troubled frown turned the corners of his lips down.

"Come on, Evie. Let's get you back to town," he said.

He took her arm in a steadying grip that she was too sensible to resist. When she swung herself on to the seat behind him, she bit down on her lip to suppress a whimper of pain.

The trip back to town seemed to last forever. Some clouds had moved in, and the sun was hidden behind them for ever increasing intervals. Even her jeans and heavy ski jacket were not enough protection from the chill of the wind, and soon she was trembling from the cold.

She sat outside on a bench while Mase returned the snowmobile. Darkness was falling quickly, and the multi-colored Christmas lights of the town had already come on. Evie concentrated on the scene before her and tried to block out the familiar, gnawing discomfort.

"Evie?" he said, watching her from the doorway.

"Ready to go?" she asked, forcing herself up off the bench.

"Why don't you wait here, and I'll go get my truck," he suggested.

"To go a few blocks down the street? Don't be ridiculous. I can walk."

"But you're in pain."

"I'm a little uncomfortable," she corrected. "Mase, it's okay. I've lived with this for years. It's no big deal. Come on, let's go."

He watched helplessly as she limped ahead of him up the street. He would gladly carry her, if she would let him, but he knew what her answer would be before he even offered.

Evie tried without success to walk normally. She hated the limp with a passion. By giving in to it, she felt that she was displaying weakness.

If her injury had happened some other way, if it had been the "accident" she had always claimed it was, then perhaps she wouldn't feel like this.

As they approached the restaurant, Evie was puzzled to see lights shining out of the window. They were closed tonight, and her employees all had the night off. A sudden quiver of apprehension went through her. Something must be wrong. Ignoring the pain, her pace increased.

They circled around the building. Lights blazed there, also. She grasped the doorknob, and found it unlocked. When she started to pull it open, Mase stayed her hand.

"Just a minute, honey," he whispered urgently.

"You can't go barging right in. You don't know who might be in there."

She glanced up at him, and in the fading light of dusk his face held a hard, uncompromising expression that was alien to her. For one, heart-stopping moment, he seemed like a stranger.

When he caught her worried gaze, his face softened slightly. He drew her away from the door, and motioned for her to stay there.

For such a large man, he could move very quickly and quietly, she observed. He eased the door open and slipped inside. Almost at once, he disappeared from sight.

Several minutes passed, and he did not reappear. She hesitated. Mase had been so emphatic about staying out here, but what if there was someone inside. What if they had hurt him?

She took a deep, sustaining breath, and quietly inched the door open. The usually neat kitchen looked as though a tornado had swept through it. Furniture was turned over, dishes were smashed, and flour was scattered over everything.

She heard a noise and whirled around. To her relief, it was Liesel that she found standing there.

"Liesel, what's going on?" she asked, a slight quaver in her voice. "Why are you here tonight?"

"The sheriff called Ben and me and told us someone had broken into the restaurant. Ve just got here a few minutes ago."

"Where's Mase?"

"In dere, with Ben," she said, pointing toward the dining room.

Evie turned and started in that direction.

"No, Evie, please. Don't go in there."

She ignored the entreaty. Angling around the worst of the mess, she made her way over to the doorway. She was filled with a deep sense of foreboding.

"Evie," Mase called. "Stay with Liesel, honey."

She froze, staring blindly into the ruined room. The same havoc had been wreaked there as in the kitchen, but that was not what stole the breath from her lungs.

Words had been scrawled across the walls. Ugly words, filled with a hate that chilled her to the marrow of her bones. She wanted to turn away, but the sight held her with a kind of horrified fascination. Her legs grew shaky, and she wondered absently, if they would continue to hold her up.

Then Mase was there. His big body blocked out the sight as he pulled her firmly into his arms. Evie buried her face against the reassuring hardness of his chest.

For long moments, her head swam sickeningly. She clung to Mase, absorbing his strength, and willing it to fill her trembling body, to chase out the dread that paralyzed her.

This was nothing but vandalism, she tried to convince herself. It was a random act of maliciousness. She watched the news. She knew that things like this happened all the time. So why did she feel instinctively that this was something personal, a blow aimed directly at her?

She heard a voice and knew someone was talking to her. Reluctantly, she drew back slightly from Mase, giving her head a small shake to clear it.

"I'm sorry, what?" she asked.

"I said not to worry," Ben's rough voice came from behind her. "We'll have this cleaned up in time to open day after tomorrow."

"The sheriff called you?" she asked, turning toward the older man. "What happened?"

"Some kids, we figure," he replied dourly. "Must have known we were closed today and nobody'd be around."

"Is Sheriff Anderson still here?"

"Nope. He left a few minutes before you got here. Everything's been taken care of. You just go on upstairs and let me and Liesel clean things up."

"But he must need me for the report," she faltered, glimpsing the words out of the corner of her eye.

"He said you could take care of that tomorrow during business hours. You know Andy, he doesn't like to be bothered when he's off duty."

"My apartment," she said, a horrible thought occurring to her. "Has it been ransacked, too?"

"Your apartment is fine, Evie," Liesel said from the doorway. "Ve checked it out, and nothing has been touched."

"Thank goodness for that but . . ."

"Come on, honey. There's nothing you can do here. Let me take you up to your place."

"I've got to get my restaurant straightened up," she insisted.

He muttered a brief, but violent oath.

"Your knee is hurting so bad that you can barely walk. What do you think you can do down here?"

Her eyes wandered back to the obscenities on the wall, and a tremor ran through her.

"Damn it to hell," he exploded, sweeping her up in his arms. "You're going up to bed, and I won't listen to any more nonsensical arguments."

"Yes, Evie. Please go with him," Liesel urged. "Ve can handle things down here."

"Okay," she agreed, knowing Mase would not give her any other choice. "Thanks Liesel. Thanks Ben."

If she were being honest with herself, she would admit that she was very glad to be leaving the wanton destruction behind her, Evie thought to herself. Her knee was throbbing miserably, and an answering ache was niggling at the back of her eyes.

She wrapped her arms around Mase's neck and allowed her head to drop on to his sturdy shoulder. His arms tightened around her in response to her implicit surrender.

The quiet solitude of her apartment was very welcome. Mase found his way through the darkened living room and into the bedroom without mishap. He set her down on the edge of the bed and fumbled for the switch of her bedside lamp.

The subdued glow illuminated her wan, pain-etched face. She sat with her shoulders slumped, trying to summon up the energy to take off her boots.

Without speaking, Mase knelt on the hard wood

floor and did it for her. He looked up at her, his bottle green eyes alight with concern.

"Thanks, Mase," she managed a slight smile. "I'll be fine now. You don't have to worry about me any more."

"Who do you think you're kidding?" he asked huskily. "You're too tired to even get undressed. No way I'm leaving you tonight, honey. Do you have anything to take for your knee?"

"I don't need anything," she replied unconvincingly.

"Like hell you don't," he said without rancor. "Now are you going to tell me, or do I go search your medicine cabinet?"

"I have some pills," she admitted reluctantly. "But I don't like to take them. They make me too groggy."

"Well that shouldn't make any difference tonight, since you're just going to bed anyway."

"But I can't be too out of it, Mase," she protested. "What if those people come back?"

"I'll be very surprised if they do, but *if* they do, *I'll* be here to deal with them."

He rose and moved purposefully into the bathroom. A moment later, he emerged with a glass of water in one hand, and two potent white pills resting on the palm of the other hand.

She ventured a glance at Mase from under her lashes. When she saw the mulish expression in his eyes, she sighed softly in resignation. Giving in to the inevitable, she accepted the pills and swallowed them with a gulp of the tepid water.

"Do you want to take a bath?" he asked.

"I think I'm too tired," she admitted.

"How about some dinner?"

"I'm not hungry," she dismissed the suggestion, her stomach doing flip flops at the thought of food.

"You should probably try to have something, Evie," he coaxed. "I don't think it's a good idea to take those pills on an empty stomach. How about a bowl of soup? It might warm you up, too."

"I suppose so," she conceded. "I think there's a couple of cans in the cupboard beside the stove."

"I'll be right back," he promised.

Evie forced herself to her feet and hobbled slowly into the bathroom. After washing her face and combing out her hair, she grabbed the night-gown that was hanging on the back of the bath-room door and went back to lie down on the bed.

When Mase returned with the steaming mug of soup, she had to confess that it smelled good. He set it on the table beside the bed and helped her slide up to lean against the fluffy pillows.

By the time she finished eating, the pills were taking effect. A warm, slightly muzzy feeling cushioned her senses, and the pain in her knee had decreased considerably.

"Let's get you into this nightgown, honey," Mase said.

He forced his hands to remain gentle and imper-sonal as he eased her out of her jeans and sweater, but when he removed her lacy bra and panties, his eyes drank in the darkly shadowed curves of her full breasts and rounded hips.

He thrust the soft folds of her old flannel night-gown over her head, both disappointed and re-lieved when she slid her arms into the sleeves like an obedient little girl.

His hot, lascivious imaginings died an instant death. This was not the time to let his libido take over. Evie needed him.

He helped her slide between the comfort of the cool sheets, and tucked her in. Her eyes were deceptively soft and slumberous as she looked up at him.

"Is there anything else we can do for your knee?" he asked, brushing a tumbled curl back from her face.

"Sometimes using a heating pad helps."

After a search, he finally located it in the hall closet. He lifted the covers and propped her knee up with a pillow, laying the heating pad beneath it.

"Is there a doctor in town that you can see tomorrow?" he asked, worrying that their outing had caused real damage to her knee.

"It won't be necessary. This has happened lots of times before. I just stayed out in the cold for too long, and it stiffened up on me. I should have known better, but I was having such a good time, I didn't want to come home.

"By morning it will be just fine. Don't worry, Mase."

"If you say so," he said doubtfully. "I guess I'll go take a shower now. Try to go to sleep."

Evie was tired and growing more drowsy by the minute, but the thought of Mase's hard, naked body under a spray of steaming water drove all thought of sleep from her mind. A deep, musical sound came from behind the partially closed door. She smiled softly, realizing that he was singing, more than slightly out of tune, in her shower. Soon that hard, muscular body would lie beside hers in her bed.

He had been so tender tonight, so concerned. She had never known much consideration from a man before. In truth, she had not believed the male of the species was capable of it. Even Uncle Jock, whom she loved dearly, did not know how to deal with a woman who was ill or in pain.

It was yet another side to Mase that she had never imagined was there. Evie was beginning to suspect that the men she had encountered so far in her life had been essentially one dimensional. But Mase was a man of many facets. She was intrigued by the idea of discovering each and every one of them.

She was so caught up in her thoughts that she did not hear him leave the bathroom and walk over to the bed. It was only when the bed dipped precariously under his weight, that she became aware of him once again.

He slid under the covers to lie close beside her. The heat of his big body traversed the small distance between them, and she was comforted by it. Her nose twitched slightly as she caught the scent of her perfumed soap, and she smiled, feeling very secure next to her lilac scented protector.

Evie reached out her hand until it brushed against the back of his. Their fingers entwined, as they fell into a deep, exhausted slumber.

NINE

As Evie predicted, her knee was almost as good as new by the following morning. She and Mase spent most of the day cleaning up the remains of the previous night's destruction. The only thing that was not salvageable was the many broken dishes. All in all, Evie considered herself lucky.

That night, she took Mase to her favorite Italian restaurant for pizza to thank him for his help. The short, stocky proprietor came charging up to them, startling Mase by encompassing Evie in an affectionate bear hug.

If the man had not been all of seventy years old, Mase would definitely have taken offense. As it was, he stood back and waited for an explanation.

"Papa, I'd like you to meet my friend, Mase. Mase, this is Papa Mario. He makes the best Italian food you've ever tasted."

Beaming at her praise, Papa shook Mase's hand vigorously before escorting them to the best table in the house.

"I thought we were just going out for pizza," Mase whispered when Papa's back was turned.

"If you want pizza, this is the only place in town," she replied. "This is a small town, remember?"

Under Papa's watchful eye, they ordered a bottle of chianti to go with their pizza. When he hustled off to get the wine, Mase sat back and took in the surroundings.

The restaurant, like many businesses in town, had once been a house. Situated on a small side street, it was accessible, but still quiet. Heavy red velvet drapes hung at the windows, and tables were topped by traditional red-and-white checkered tablecloths. The chairs were bare wood, but comfortable.

"Why do I get the feeling that he's staring at me, even when his back is turned?" Mase inquired wryly.

"Sorry," Evie apologized with a self-conscious laugh. "I'm afraid you'll just have to accept the fact that any man I'm seen with is food for gossip. They never *do* see me with men, you see."

"Never?" he repeated, raising an eyebrow in disbelief.

"Well, never with a foreigner."

"Foreigner? We didn't cross over some border that night during the storm, did we? I mean, the last time I looked, we were in the United States."

"Sometimes I wonder. Especially during the winter when we're so cut off from the outside world. It seems like we live in a world of our own.

"It's a very peaceful, pleasant little place. Sometimes I'd like to forget that the real world exists."

"That world can be a nice place, too," Mase reasoned.

"Maybe," Evie admitted. "But it never seemed that way to me. I think I prefer my own little world."

"Like Sleeping Beauty."

"What do you mean?"

"She was safe and secure, sleeping her life away in her own little world. The only catch was that she wasn't really living. She just existed."

Perhaps it was fortunate that Papa interrupted them at that point with the arrival of their wine. The two men were occupied with the wine-pouring ceremony, allowing Evie time to consider his words.

Existing. Was that all she was doing? Her world seemed so full. Was she really missing out on life?

They sat silently over their wine for a time, exquisitely aware of the rich, spicy aroma of their baking pizza and the muffled noises from the kitchen. Several long moments passed and a handsome young man with dark eyes came to stand close by and serenade them with his violin.

The haunting melodies of the soft Italian love songs that he played made Evie feel inexplicably lonely. Her hand stretched across the table toward his, and Mase's thumb caressed her palm.

They rose as one, and their feet carried them to the tiny wooden dance floor in the back of the restaurant. Evie melted into the cradle of his arms as if it had been made especially for her. Her head rested on the broad hardness of his chest. One hand was clasped in his, and Mase's arm encircled her protectively.

Mama appeared in the doorway to the kitchen, carrying their dinner on a large tray, but Papa stopped her.

"Keep it warm for them," Papa whispered, a knowing look warming his dark eyes. "It is better that they dance now."

By the time they had finished their dinner, it was much too late to see the movie as they had planned. Other diners had come and gone, but they troubled Mase and Evie not at all.

They strolled along the fairy-tale street hand in hand. Mase brushed the snow off a park bench and they sat without speaking, warmed by each other's presence despite the freezing temperatures. When they finally climbed up the stairs to Evie's door, she turned to face him with the key clasped in her hand.

"Mase, I'm really tired. If you don't mind, I'll say good night here."

"Tired?" he questioned softly, his green eyes seeming to penetrate her soul.

"Tired . . . and a little confused."

"All right, love," he acquiesced. "But don't expect me to leave without a good-night kiss."

"Who says I'd want you to."

Her lips were icy from the cold night air, as were his, but the instant spark of chemistry between them heated that cold flesh to the melting point in a matter of seconds. A light fall of snowflakes swirled around them, landing in their hair and catching on their eyelashes.

When they parted, the longing in Mase's eyes was mirrored in Evie's. He drew her gloved fingers to his lips, and the heat of his breath warmed them.

"Will I see you tomorrow?" she asked hopefully.

"If you want to."

"Oh, yes, I want to." She shook her head slightly, as if to clear it, and stepped back against the door.

"I was going to get my Christmas tree tomorrow," she said. "Would you like to come along and help me pick one out? I'll make us some dinner and we can trim it tomorrow night."

"I'd like that very much."

"Would two o'clock be all right?"

"I'll be here. Good night, Evie. Sweet dreams."

When she stepped into her apartment, it was totally dark. The darkness took Evie by surprise, because she always left a light on when she went out at night. She guessed it must have blown out.

She made her way over to the floor lamp by feel. When she touched it, the stem of the lamp was still warm. She flipped the switch, and the light blazed to life.

She blinked at the sudden brightness, trying to focus her eyes on the familiar room. Little things that were not as they should be, caught her attention.

The afghan that covered her ancient sofa was

always smoothed neatly over the lumpy cushions, but tonight it was slightly rumpled. An empty glass sat on the coffee table in front of it, and Evie never left dishes sitting in the living room.

She strained her ears for a sound, anything that would tell her that she was not alone, but there was nothing.

She took a deep, sustaining breath, and moved forward, throwing the closet door open. The light came on automatically, revealing the familiar cubicle filled with her neatly hung clothes. Everything was in place. There was no bogeyman awaiting her.

A long, slow breath escaped her lungs. Evie searched quickly through the closet, trying to find something, anything that she could use as a weapon. An umbrella was the first thing her questing hands discovered, and she picked it up, not stopping to question its effectiveness. She tiptoed into the next room.

A thorough search revealed nothing. Who could have been here? she asked herself nervously. If it were not for the glass on the coffee table, she would have thought the whole incident had been her imagination.

Shivers coursed through her body just as they had on the stormy night when she had first met Mase. Evie pulled the thick down quilt off the bed and wrapped herself snugly in it. She went out into the living room, turned on all the lights, and curled up in her old-fashioned overstuffed chair.

This incident *must* be connected to what happened in her restaurant last night. She was no great believer in coincidence. She shivered, wishing vainly that Mase were with her.

Memories of the heat which radiated from his big body during the night tantalized her. He could keep her warmer than her blankets and quilt combined, she admitted to herself longingly. Warm and safe.

For years she had avoided intimacy with a man out of fear of being hurt, as she had been hurt by Allen. Logic told her that all men weren't like him, but she was afraid of making the wrong choice again.

She wasn't really afraid of the simple, physical act of making love. No, it was the implied surrender, the vulnerability, that disturbed her.

Surely, if all he cared about was having sex with her, he'd had his chance the last two nights, her logical self argued. She'd offered herself to him, but he had refused, knowing that she was not ready.

She tried to reason it out dispassionately, but there was no room for logic in the deep, dark recesses of her frightened child's mind.

She had learned early in life that there were no sure things. Did she care enough about Mase to take a chance?

Memories of his soft, caressing voice and the pleasure his strong, sensual hands had given her, returned to her in a rush. Most vivid of all was the sense of safety and security that she felt when she had lain in his arms through the long, dark night. Those memories beckoned to her, and she was filled with such a sense of longing that she knew the answer had to be yes.

The next move would be up to her. Tomorrow night would be her chance, if she didn't lose her nerve. She would have to be strong. Too much was hanging in the balance.

Early the next morning Evie set off for the nearby town of Wenatchee. She had spent the remainder of the long, sleepless night curled up in a chair, listening nervously for the intruder to return.

She greeted the pale light of dawn with a tremendous sense of relief, and she was up and out of her apartment much earlier than usual.

When she arrived in Wenatchee, she headed directly for a little shop that was next door to one of her regular suppliers. Evie had seen the shop many times, but had never had enough nerve to go in. She sat in her car for half an hour, trying to work up her courage.

A large pink neon sign on the front of the building flashed: The Love Boutique. It looked X-rated to Evie. When she tentatively opened the door, she was relieved to find that it was not a sleazy sex store, as she had feared. In fact, the sales clerk was a respectable-looking middle-aged woman.

Half an hour later, she heaved a sigh of relief and climbed back into her car, setting her package on the worn seat next to her. As she pulled out on to the highway, she said a silent prayer that she wouldn't be in an accident and be found with that suggestive, heart-covered sack by her side.

Her only other stop was at a gourmet delicatessen. There she picked up several delicacies for their supper, and a bottle of imported French champagne that cost her almost a day's profits. Well, at least a *slow* day's profits.

Throwing caution to the wind, she allowed the clerk to talk her into buying a jar of caviar. It was an extravagance she had never before permitted herself. The contents of the jar looked a bit like her homemade huckleberry preserves, but something told her that it wouldn't taste like them.

She hurried home to put the wine and perishables into the refrigerator. A quick glance at the clock told her that she barely had enough time to change her clothes before Mase arrived.

At precisely two o'clock his familiar knock sounded on the door. She opened it to find him dressed in jeans, a heavy sweater, boots, and an ancient wool jacket. He looked so handsome that he took her breath away.

"Hi," she breathed, her unconsciously seductive eyes and upturned face inviting his kiss.

It was an invitation he had no intention of refusing. Several minutes passed before either of them had breath to speak again.

Evie reluctantly pulled out of his arms and tucked her dark curls up under her tightly knit stocking cap. The smile that curved her lips was a bit rueful.

"I think we'd better go now," she said apologetically.

"I think you're right," he replied, an answering

smile lighting his deep green eyes. "Where do you find trees around here?"

"Need you ask?" she inquired mischievously, pointing to the axe which was resting against a nearby wall.

Mase turned to follow her pointing finger and groaned. "I should have guessed."

"You really don't have to do it, Mase," Evie said, managing to look a bit pathetic. "We could just get a tree up at the Safeway store. Of course, it will be a little old and dried out and they're always shaped so that you can hardly hang an ornament on them. But I don't want you to do anything you don't want to do."

"Okay," he said, resigned to his fate. "We'll go cut one down."

"Thanks, Mase," she replied, tugging at the front of his coat until he bent down and she could throw her arms around his neck.

"Evie, you've got two choices."

"I do?"

"Yup. You can either grab that axe and go get your tree right now or spend the rest of the day here." Mase glanced down at her. "I think you'd better make that the rest of the week."

"I can take a hint," she said, pulling herself out of his arms once more and reaching for the axe. "Let's go."

"I was afraid you'd say that."

The snow had started to fall again. Huge, feathery flakes drifted to earth, leaving their lacy white covering on the darkness of the newly cleared walkways and streets. Mase and Evie made their way cautiously down her stairway and around the building to Mase's gun-metal gray pickup.

The old engine rumbled to life, and the wipers soon cleared away the whiteness that had collected on the windshield. Evie was surprised by the blast of warm air that blew out around her legs.

"You got your heater fixed," she exclaimed.

"I thought it would make it more comfortable if we were stranded out in the wilderness again."

"It won't be that bad," she promised, a smile lurking behind her eyes. "It's just a tree farm a couple of miles out of town."

Mase and Evie walked along row after row of trees, debating the merits of one over another until they finally found one that was acceptable to both of them.

Reinforced by the power of Mase's huge torso, the axe took only a few blows to chop down the tree. They shook the dry, powdery snow from its branches before settling it into the back of his truck.

When they arrived back in town, Mase parked as close to Evie's stairs as possible. He lifted the heavier trunk end easily while Evie led the way, supporting the tree's top.

She produced a bright red-and-green tree stand, and together they managed to set up the beautiful seven-foot-high Grand fir.

"Give me your coat and I'll hang it up," Evie offered. "You can put your boots over there by the radiator to dry with mine."

"It's kind of cold in here," Mase observed. "How about if I start a fire?"

"That would be great. I'll just be a few minutes. I'm going to change my clothes."

Evie hurried into the bathroom and locked the door, stripping off her plain, utilitarian clothes with fingers that trembled. She donned the tiniest of transparent ice-blue bikini panties which tied with little satin bows at her hips, a matching demi-cup bra, and a lacy little garter belt.

She had never worn anything like them before, and she had to make several attempts before she got the seams straight on the sheer silk stockings. When she straightened up, her eyes found her reflection in the full-length mirror on her door. Those eyes grew wide as they took in every detail of the wanton stranger before her.

Evie squared her shoulders and reached for the small bottle of her favorite perfume which stood beside the sink. She dabbed it behind her ears and on her wrists, and, daringly, between her breasts.

Before she could change her mind, she slipped into the blouse and skirt that she had hung on the bathroom door that morning. She ran a brush through her long hair, which she left loose around her shoulders, slid her feet into the strappy silver slippers, and went out to join Mase.

He smiled appreciatively at the sight of her in a soft, sapphire-blue skirt that clung temptingly to her womanly hips and the pleasing roundness of her derriere. The matching blouse of sheer silk had fine silver threads running through it. The sleeves were long and full, cuffed at her delicate wrists, and the neckline plunged low enough to display quite a bit of cleavage.

One feathery curl rested enticingly on the full curve of her breast. Mase's eyes fastened on it and he burned with desire to feel that silky flesh once again.

"Would you like to put the lights on the tree while I start dinner?" she asked, gesturing to the box of decorations beside the sofa.

"Fine," he replied absently.

What was wrong with him, he wondered in frustration. He had never before pursued a woman this way. In truth, he had never had to. Mase was not a conceited man, but he could not help but be aware that he was attractive to women.

They tended to pursue *him* rather than the other way around. Perhaps it was the novelty of being rejected that intrigued him, he speculated. But no, it was more than that. He could hardly keep his hands off Evie, and despite her hesitation, he knew she enjoyed his touch.

The other night had been a new experience for him. He had never before concentrated all his energy on giving pleasure without expecting to receive it as well. He had never wanted a woman more than he had wanted Evie that night, and he knew that she would have allowed him to take her, but he wanted more than just her acquiescence. He wanted her to burn for him, as he did for her.

He watched her as she bustled around the tiny kitchen, and wondered just what there was about her that attracted him. She was beautiful, of course. Her slim figure was nicely rounded in all the right places, her skin was soft and smooth. Her eyes were a clear silvery gray, and when she smiled, as she often did, they glowed with the luminescence of wintry moonlight.

Mase had known many beautiful women in his time, but none had inspired the emotions he experienced around Evie. There was an air of innocence and vulnerability about her that made him long to guard her from the cold cruelties of the world.

"Mase?" she questioned from the doorway, puzzled by his withdrawal.

"Sorry, honey, did you say something?"

"I just wondered if you wanted a drink."

"Whatever you're having will be fine."

Evie went back into the kitchen and poured two glasses of dry white wine into elegant cut crystal glasses. She glanced over at Mase, watching him work the strings of colored lights in amongst the branches. Her eyes went back to the wine. She took a deep breath and downed half of hers in three gulps.

She glanced furtively at Mase, but he was so engrossed in putting on the lights that he hadn't noticed what she had done. She refilled her glass and joined him in the living room.

"Do you need some help?"

"No thanks," he replied. "I'm almost done."

A few minutes later he plopped down beside her on the couch and took his drink.

"I don't have much experience decorating trees, but I think I got the lights spaced pretty evenly," he said, sipping the drink appreciatively.

"They look great to me," she encouraged. "What comes next?"

They went to work hanging glittery balls, some new and some very old, on strategic limbs around the tree. Evie picked up an old gold carousel horse and hung it tenderly on a sturdy branch near a gold light bulb. Next came a clip-on bird with a tattered tinsel tail.

"I always hang this box first so that they get the best places on the tree. Then we can fill in with the others. These ornaments belonged to my aunt and uncle. They gave me a box when I went away to college," she explained.

With that pleasant task completed, they began the time-consuming job of hanging the sparkling strands of tinsel. The finishing touch was a blue foil star with an angel in the center.

"I guess you get to put the top on," she said with a sigh. "It's too high for me."

"That's easy enough to take care of," he replied.

His strong hands grasped her tiny waist and lifted her up within easy reach of the tree's top. When she settled the star in its place, he eased her down against his chest, holding her there with her feet dangling a good foot off the floor.

"Umm, you taste as good as you look," Mase said, dipping his head to nuzzle at the sensitive cords of her neck.

"Mase, put me down," she ordered. "I don't appreciate being hung here like . . . like an ornament on the tree."

"Your wish is my command, my lady," he said, swinging her up in his arms.

He sat down on the easy chair, snuggling her on his lap. His large hand cupped the back of her head and he ran his fingers teasingly through her silky curls. His warm lips closed over hers as his free hand palmed a silk-covered breast.

Evie's legs curled up instinctively and that hand moved to knead the calf of her leg with seductive intent, creeping slyly upward. Evie knew the time wasn't right, but she couldn't bring herself to stop him.

In the end, it took the shrill whistle of the long-simmering tea kettle to penetrate the sensual fog that surrounded them. Mase's lips reluctantly lifted from hers, and for a long, poignant moment, they simply stared into each other's eyes with undisguised longing.

"I guess you're saved by the bell, so to speak," Mase said as he released her.

Once she was safe out in the kitchen, Evie straightened her tousled hair and dished up two plates of savory chicken and dumplings. When she carried them out into the living room, Mase plugged in the tree lights and they sat side by side in the half-darkened room, eating with their plates in their laps.

"It's a beautiful tree, isn't it?" Evie asked, toying with a bite of fluffy dumpling.

"Yes, it is."

A few minutes later, she picked up their plates and started out into the kitchen. Mase's was satisfyingly empty, but Evie had been unable to eat.

The moment was rapidly approaching, and her anxiety was growing by leaps and bounds.

"Would you like another drink?" she asked.

"No thanks."

Evie sat down very close to Mase and held a small sprig of mistletoe over his head. She gathered the shreds of her courage around her. It was now or never.

"Well, well, well, what have we here?" she teased nervously.

"Looks suspiciously like mistletoe to me," he returned, wondering what she was up to. "What are we going to do about it?"

"We-lll," she drawled. "I'd hate to break a tradition, especially at Christmastime. I mean, it might be bad luck or something."

"It's sure to be," he agreed. "After all, Santa Claus is watching. You might end up with nothing but a lump of coal in your stocking."

"I think it's only fair to warn you that this isn't ordinary mistletoe, Mase," she murmured, rising up on her knees and leaning down over him.

"It's not?"

"Nope. It's imported French mistletoe, so the custom is a little different."

"Never let it be said that Mason Kincaid is narrow-minded," he said, a small flicker of excitement showing in his eyes. "I put myself completely in your hands."

Her trembling fingers slowly unfastened the buttons of his shirt, baring the broad expanse of his hard, manly chest. Those fingers were icy with nervousness as they tentatively caressed his heated flesh, and he drew in a sharp breath at the contact.

"I'm afraid my hands are a little cold," she apologized, blowing into his ear.

"I can easily warm them up," he promised, reaching out to draw her closer.

"Oh no you don't," she said, holding him off determinedly. "You're the one who's under the mistletoe. You're the *kissee,* not the *kisser.*"

"All right, I give up. Do with me as you will."

Evie pushed his shirt off his brawny shoulders and laid it over the back of the couch. She crept still closer, bending down to cover his lips with her own.

Her body was slightly stiff at first, but she soon relaxed enough to slip on to his lap, molding herself to his muscular form. His lips parted readily under her hesitant probing, urging her to go a step further.

Evie felt awkward as she slipped her tongue into his mouth. Mase seized it at once, sucking it lightly, coaxing her to explore the hot, damp secrets of his mouth.

Long moments later, she drew back to scatter seductive little kisses along the hard line of his sun-darkened throat and across his broad shoulders to his massive, hair-covered chest.

Evie was all too warm now, as her slim, supple fingers stroked and caressed his responsive flesh. Her tongue darted out to taste the warm, slightly salty skin of his smoothly muscled shoulder, and she felt Mase start violently in reaction.

He drew in his breath sharply, his entire body

going rigid. With almost superhuman strength of will, he grasped her waist and set her off his lap.

"Evie, I'm warning you, if you aren't serious you'd better run for your life, because I can't stand any more. It's all I can do to keep from throwing you down on the floor and taking you right now."

She hesitated for a long moment, then rose, moving away from him. Mase closed his eyes, trying to fight back the throbbing desire that was almost a physical pain. When he opened his eyes again, he could hardly believe what he was seeing.

With slow, sensual deliberation, Evie unfastened the buttons of her blouse. Her fingers seemed to work with a will of their own, and her eyes never left his. She shrugged the wisp of silk off her shoulders and it floated lightly to the floor. Her trembling fingers moved on to the waistband of her skirt.

It followed the path of her blouse, lying in a dark puddle at her feet. She stepped slowly out of it, kicking off her little silver slippers at the same time.

"God," he said, almost to himself. "Those little blue wisps of nothing are the sexiest things I've ever seen."

She stood as still a statue except for the tumultuous rise and fall of her breasts and faced him nervously. He rose and stood before her, so close that she could feel the heat of his body, but not his touch.

"Tell me what you want, Evie. I need to hear you say the words."

She swallowed the lump in her throat before

answering. "I want you to make love to me, Mase."

A wave of pure masculine need swept over him as she spoke. He lifted her up in his arms, carrying her across the room to settle her against the soft sheepskin throw before the blazing fire. He stood confidently, silhouetted by the bright orangy glow, and undressed, just as he had that first night.

But tonight Evie did not have the protective veil of the shadows to shield her from the sight of his nakedness. Tonight she would know all there was to know about Mase's big, masculine body.

Evie was so lost in her thoughts that she was startled when he knelt beside her and raised her slightly to unhook her bra. The straps of the lacy garment slid slowly down her arms to be tossed aside.

It wasn't so bad, she tried to convince herself. It was nothing he hadn't already seen. Even that comforting rationalization deserted her as he untied the little bows of her panties and drew them off, exposing the last secret of her body to his hot, hungry gaze.

She wished he would finish the job and take off her garter belt and stockings, too. Embarrassment flooded over her as she thought of how she must look.

The sheer size of him, along with the heated desire in his eyes, caused a shiver of fright to pass through her. What if she was wrong about him? What if he really was like Allen?

Her slender frame was cast into shadow as the bulk of Mase's body descended on her, blotting out the light and heat of the fire and replacing it with the heat of his desire. As his weight pressed down upon her, it was all she could do to keep from struggling against him.

Mase sensed the fear in the cold, still little body beneath his. He rolled over on his side, his arms encircling her as he cuddled her to him. His fingers combed through her long hair, one hand stroking soothingly along her satiny back as he pressed soft kisses up her throat and along the soft curve of her cheek.

"It's all right, love," he murmured. "Just relax."

The gentle caresses continued for what seemed an eternity. After a time, when he did nothing more, Evie sighed and some of the tension left her body.

"Evie?" he questioned hesitantly. "There's something I need to know. Are you a virgin?"

"No," she whispered, her voice so soft that he had to strain to hear her.

Mase could feel the tension tightening her muscles once again. Although he held her body close, he sensed that she was retreating from him emotionally.

"I'm glad," he replied.

The unexpectedness of his words startled Evie, and her eyes flew to his face. Her confusion was obvious, and Mase raised his hand to trace the full curve of her lips.

"Why?" she questioned in bewilderment. "I thought men liked the idea of being the first."

"I'm glad because I don't want to hurt you,

and even with the most careful lover, there's some pain the first time.''

His face grew taut as he watched the play of emotions that crossed her delicate features. Strong arms tightened protectively around her.

"Your first lover wasn't careful, was he?'' he pressed.

Her silence was his reply.

"It's all right, love,'' he murmured. "This time will be different. You weren't afraid when I pleasured you the other morning, were you?''

She shook her head against his shoulder.

"Well, what I'm going to do tonight won't be that much different. I'll just be using another part of my body to give us *both* pleasure. We'll go slow and easy. Nothing will happen until you're ready for it, and if I do anything you don't like, or anything that frightens you, just tell me and I'll stop. You're in control, Evie. Remember that.''

She gradually relaxed under his gentle ministrations, and as the stiffness left her body, she began to tremble. His mouth traveled lower, across the soft slope of her shoulders to nuzzle gently at the beginning swell of her breasts.

His big hand cupped the tender flesh of one soft mound, playing with it until she whimpered and clutched at his broad back. Mase's mouth closed over her straining nipple and his tongue teased and tormented it deliciously. Evie moved restlessly under him, and he moved lower, crawling down her body as he spread warm, damp kisses over her abdomen.

Another shiver coursed through her, but this

time it was one of sheer pleasure. Mase's hands and lips and tongue evoked sensations that filled Evie with a warm glow, but at the same time, made her feel achingly empty. It was an emptiness only Mase could fill.

One hand slipped between her thighs, exploring, tantalizing, until she writhed beneath him, and a sudden dampness met his bold fingers. Her nails dug into his skin as tremors shook her, and a series of breathy moans escaped her throat.

"That's right, love," he said, his voice deep and filled with satisfaction. "You're ready for me now, aren't you? Tell me that you're ready."

"Yes," she breathed, her voice echoing both her confusion and her need. "Oh yes, please."

"Then show me where you want me, Evie."

Her legs parted in invitation and he slid between them, his manhood probing the threshold to her sweet warmth. He paused for a moment before seeking entry, and she stiffened once again.

"Put your arms around my neck," he whispered into her mouth. "I promised it wouldn't hurt, love, and you know I always keep my promises."

She obeyed, and gently, with infinite care, he drove himself home. Her eyes widened and she gasped, overwhelmed by the sensations she experienced. As Mase had promised, there was no pain, only an immense fullness. And pleasure. Such pleasure that it took her breath away.

Mase held himself still at first, allowing her to adjust to his entry, even though his instincts cried out in protest. He was on fire with his need for her, but he forced himself to wait until she was ready. Finally, unable to hold back any longer, his lean hips began to rotate slowly against hers. The shock of his entry faded and was gone, and the hunger returned a hundredfold.

He began to thrust into her with deep, leisurely strokes calculated to drive her crazy. Evie wrapped her slender thighs around his hips and arched instinctively into his thrusts.

His hands and lips seemed to be everywhere at once, and the plethora of sensations she experienced rocked her to the very core of her being. Reality faded before the onslaught of pleasure. Mase was her only stability, her anchor in the face of the wild, swirling sea of passion that threatened to engulf her. She clung to him tightly, afraid of losing herself forever in that churning morass.

Her body was stretched taut, like a bowstring that was about to snap. She yearned for it, struggled toward it, for therein was her release from the sensual prison in which she was being held.

"Please, Mase . . . please," she sobbed.

Mase quickened his pace, and all at once, the world burst in upon her. Mase's body convulsed, and she realized that he had followed her into that magical world of fulfillment.

When he finally came back down to earth, Mase was instantly aware of the small, fragile body beneath his, and he rolled on his side, carrying Evie with him. She curled up against him and buried her face under his chin.

Evie didn't know what to say or do. She couldn't express in words the things she was feeling. Should she remain silent, as Mase was doing? Something told her that he was waiting for her to speak.

"I can hear your heart beating," she said at last, threading her fingers through the crisp, curling hair on his damp chest.

"Can you? What does it sound like?"

"It sounds strong and steady, and very wonderful. Just like you." She raised her head and their eyes met for a long moment.

"My turn now," he said, rolling her over on her back and laying his ear against her chest.

"What does mine sound like?"

"Thump . . . thump . . . thump . . ." he said, slyly capturing her nipple and teasing it with long, calloused fingers. "Thumpthumpthump," he went on.

"Hey," she protested. "That's not fair."

"You know what they say. 'All's fair in love.' "

"You mean 'All's fair in love *and war*.' "

"No, I don't. I've never felt less like making war in my life."

"You don't have to make war. I've already surrendered to the superior force."

"Evie . . ." he protested, his arms tightening around her. "I never tried to force you into anything. I wanted it to be your decision."

"Shh," she replied, tenderly brushing the perspiration-dampened hair back off his forehead and cradling his head to her breasts. "That's not what I meant. I was talking about the force of need, of desire, of . . ." She stopped short of saying love.

His body relaxed again, and a hard, muscular thigh slid between hers. He nuzzled the soft hollow between her breasts, his tongue tasting the delicate, womanly flavor of her.

"I love the smell of your perfume. You always smell like honey and wildflowers and the sweetest of ripe summer fruit. It makes me want to take a bite to see if you taste as good as you smell." His teeth nipped playfully at the round underside of a breast.

"What big teeth you have, Grandmother," she teased, nipping at the hard muscles of his shoulder in return.

"Honey, if I remind you of your grandmother, there's definitely something wrong with my technique."

"Maybe it just needs . . . Oh!" she cried out in surprise as his hair-roughened thigh began rubbing temptingly against her feminine softness.

"You were saying?" he asked smugly.

"Maybe you need to . . . to practice your technique a little," she panted. "I'm more than willing to help."

Words became impossible as he levered his hard body up over her once again, starting them back on the road to ecstasy.

TEN

The fire had died down to deep, burnished coals and the room had grown cold. Evie stirred in Mase's arms and he instantly came awake.

"What time is it?" she asked sleepily.

He shifted her slightly, lifting his arm so that he could see his watch. She stretched like a contented kitten.

"It's just after two."

"Umm. I guess we'd better unplug the tree lights and go to bed."

"I suppose so. Do you want me to leave?" he asked reluctantly.

"Just try it," she threatened complacently. "I'm perfectly willing to tie you to the bed to keep you here. Don't make me get physical."

"Honey, I'd go to almost any lengths to make you get physical," he replied, looking down at his sleepy little tigress with affection.

When they rose from the floor, Mase stood in front of her with his hands resting on her hips. He did not speak, and when Evie looked up into his eyes, her own reflected a wealth of emotions.

"As sexy as these things are," he said at last, running a finger under the top of her garter belt, "I think we can do without them now."

One by one he released the hooks which held her stockings up, allowing the bits of smoky silk to fall to the floor. His fingers fumbled for the clasp that opened the lacy blue belt. A moment later he tossed it aside and bent to peel the stockings off her feet.

He pressed hot kisses up along both legs to the juncture of her thighs. Her knees grew almost too weak to support her as his kisses grew more and more intimate. She reached down to clasp his shoulders to steady herself.

"Time for bed, love," he whispered, feeling a hot shaft of desire pierce him once again.

Evie did not waste her time putting on a nightgown which she knew Mase would soon take off anyway. The bed was cold and damp against her naked body. She started to shiver, but he soon joined her, warming her with the heat of his body, just as she had imagined he could.

He started his seduction of her senses again, and this time she surrendered with a blissful sigh. She wondered if it were possible to die of pleasure.

When Mase awoke again, early-morning sunshine lit the room. Evie was still abandoned to sleep, curled trustingly along his side with her head pillowed on his shoulder. A wily smile curved his lips, and he reached behind her to tickle the small of her back.

She moaned in protest, turning over on her back without waking. Pleased with his success, Mase eased the quilt away from her, leaving her naked and exposed to the brilliant sunlight that reflected off the newly fallen snow.

He supported his brawny torso on his elbow, enjoying the unobstructed view of her body's pink-and-white perfection. The fact that it was only perfect to his biased eyes did not occur to him. The small scar on her abdomen from a long-past appendectomy and the little heart-shaped strawberry birthmark on the inside of one breast, only served to endear her to him.

He decided that the dim, artificial light of the evening had not done justice to the full roundness of her coral-tipped breasts. The cold air caused goose bumps to rise on her soft, smooth skin, and her nipples grew taut, as though his intent gaze was a physical caress.

Her waist was tiny and her abdomen flat, but her hips and thighs were nicely rounded. The sight made him wonder why he'd always thought he liked women who were pencil thin. Evie's fuller figure was just right.

The silky hairs at the tops of her thighs stood on end as goose bumps rose there also. Mase could not resist blowing damp, teasing little breaths over them. She shifted in her sleep.

The fine white lines of several scars ran along the perimeter of one knee. Her "bad" knee, Evie had called it. He feathered a kiss over the spots which had given her pain, as though he could make it go away.

When he crawled back up to the head of the bed, he found that the rosy buds that crowned her breasts were painfully engorged. Taking pity on them, Mase flicked first one and then the other with the tip of his tongue. Evie sighed, shifting restlessly beside him.

She awoke to the exquisitely pleasurable sensation of her lover suckling at her breast. Her lover. She smiled at the thought. Mason Kincaid was her lover.

Her fingers combed through his tousled hair and he looked up to find the radiance of her smile resting on him. It warmed him more than the hottest sunlight.

"Maybe I'd better get you something more substantial in the way of breakfast," she teased.

"You're all the breakfast I need," he replied with a slow, sexy smile that did strange things to the rhythm of her pulse.

His lips and tongue and gentle teeth danced their magic back and forth across the highly sensitized globes until Evie quivered uncontrollably. Satisfied with the state of her arousal, Mase tried to nudge her legs apart, but her body went taut with pain and she sucked her breath in through her teeth. Her hands instinctively pressed against his chest.

"I'm sorry, Mase," she said in a voice that was little more than a whimper. "I don't think I can right now."

"It's all right, honey," he replied, reaching out

to gather her back into his arms. "It's been a long time for you, hasn't it?"

"Four years," she replied.

"What you need is a good long soak in a hot tub," he went on, seeming pleased by her answer. "It'll help those sore, stiff muscles relax. You just stay right here and I'll get it ready for you."

A few minutes later he returned with a large towel in his hand. He helped her sit up, and handed it to her.

"Wrap your hair up in this, Evie. It'll keep it dry."

After she had done as he directed, Mase helped her into the old footed bathtub. He stood back and enjoyed the sight of the fragrant bubbles teasing her creamy shoulders and breasts.

"I'll be back in a few minutes. Just relax for a little while."

True to his word, he returned a short time later with a tray bearing two steaming mugs and a plate of croissants. After putting down the lid, he took the only seat available and handed her a cup of coffee.

"I hope I put enough cream in your coffee," he said, his nose wrinkling at the sight of the pale beige liquid.

"It looks perfect. Those croissants look good, too," she ventured hopefully.

"Yes, they do, don't they?"

"This isn't fair, you know. I burned off a lot of calories last night. I need some sustenance."

He appeared to consider it. "Okay, I guess I can share," he finally conceded, breaking off a large bite of the roll he was eating and waving it under her nose.

She opened her mouth and he stuffed the bite of pastry into it. Her tongue darted out to catch a crumb on her upper lip, and Mase's eyes fastened hotly on the provocative movement.

"You know," she said after a moment, "this is absolutely decadent."

"I know," he replied, offering her another bite. "It's a shame we aren't at my cabin. I have a hot tub that's big enough for both of us. It's not fair for you to be decadent alone."

"I think maybe it's just as well. Can I get out now? I'll turn into a prune if I'm in here much longer."

Surrendering to that threat, he helped her out.

Evie felt much better after her bath. She slipped into her best robe and fumbled under the bed for the matching slippers. The soft mauve of the velvet robe was captured by her eyes, transforming their grayness to the color of spring lilacs.

When she joined him in the kitchen, he had dressed in his clothes from the previous night. The scattered clothes they had left before the fireplace had been picked up and neatly put away.

She might have believed that their night of passion had only been a dream if it weren't for the look in his eyes when they rested on her. That and the funny little shuffling steps she had to take to appease the throbbing ache between her legs.

"I'm afraid I don't have much to fix for breakfast."

"Didn't your plans for last night go as far as the morning after?" he teased.

"I wasn't sure there'd *be* a morning after. I mean, I wasn't sure you'd still be here this morning."

"No?" he questioned with raised brows. "I distinctly remember being threatened with physical violence if I tried to leave."

"Mase," she protested.

"Let's check this out," he said, opening the refrigerator door and peering in. "French champagne sounds like a good start for a brunch. Smoked salmon, Brie cheese. Are you sure you didn't plan for this? Just add that pear and the rest of the croissants and you've got a pretty good menu."

"Different anyway," Evie was forced to add. "What I'd planned this for was a late supper last night. The pickled asparagus and Greek olives aren't exactly breakfast fare."

"We'll save them for dinner tonight."

"I can't have dinner with you tonight, Mase," she said, a look of dismay crossing her face. "I'm afraid I have other plans for the rest of today and tonight."

"Other plans?" he echoed incredulously. "You mean as in a date?"

"Not exactly a date. I have to baby-sit."

"That's no problem. I'll just come over after they leave."

"They won't *be* leaving. I'm keeping them overnight."

"Why overnight?"

"My cousins and their husbands are going to Seattle to shop for Christmas and they're going to stay over for the night. It gives them a chance to be alone for an evening. They do this every year. I promised them weeks ago, and I can't go back on my word."

"I wouldn't ask you to, honey," he replied, feeling a bit selfish. "I know . . . I'll help you with the kids."

"I don't know if that's such a good idea," she said doubtfully.

"Why not?"

"Have you spent much time around small children?"

"No, actually I've never been around any," he replied with a lack of concern that bordered on the foolhardy in Evie's opinion. "It can't be all that hard, though. After all, they're just small people."

"All right then, yes," she said with a slightly wicked smile lilting on her lips. "I think perhaps you *should* meet my cousins' children."

At exactly nine o'clock, Evie's cousins arrived at the door of her apartment, their respective progeny in tow. Both were plump, pretty, blue-eyed blondes. They were the perfect foils for Evie's dark, sultry beauty, but Mase had the feeling that her quiet nature had always made Evie take a backseat to her cousins' vivaciousness.

There was a brief flurry of activity and the two women were gone. Mase found the three children all staring at him somberly.

"These are my cousin Jenny's kids, Katie and Jody," Evie said, breaking the silence. "And this is Susan's little Jeremy."

Mase watched with interest as Evie cuddled the ten-month-old baby in her arms. He felt eyes upon him, and turned to the two older children, crouching down to their level and smiling at them.

Apparently that smile even worked on children, Evie noted. The usually shy five-year-old twins instantly came over to him and made friendly overtures.

"Okay, troops," Evie said. "Are we going to sit here all morning or do you want to go have fun?"

"Oboy, let's go," Jody shouted, heading for the door. "Last one there's a rotten egg."

"Oh no you don't," Evie said laughingly. She caught him by the collar of his shirt just as he reached the door. "You wait right here while I get Jeremy ready. We're all going together or we're not going at all. Is that understood?"

"Yes, Aunt Evie," he sulked, eyes downcast as he studied the toe of his little snow boot.

Evie slipped her coat on and zipped it up before wrestling with the metal-framed baby carrier. With Mase's help, she finally got it settled on her back and fastened all the safety straps.

"Can you put Jeremy in for me, Mase?"

He lifted the plump, snow-suited little form and tried to settle him into the canvas sling, but twenty pounds of playfully wriggling baby managed to undermine his efforts. Exasperated, he tried to stuff the tiny, blanketed feet through the only opening he saw.

"Mister," Katie tugged relentlessly at Mase's pant leg. "Mister, you can't put both his feet through the same hole. They won't fit."

He lifted the gurgling baby back out of the carrier and held him against his shoulder as he checked out the problem. Jeremy cheerfully spit up on him.

Half an hour later, little Jeremy was safely settled in his carrier and Mase's jacket looked respectable, if not like new. They set off to explore the many pleasures of the Christmas Lighting Festival.

The town was already so crowded that they could barely move along the sidewalk, and more buses were arriving by the minute. The main street was blocked off to traffic and merrymakers roamed the town at will.

The local high school band had taken center stage in the park's bandstand, and their cheery music penetrated every area of the small town. At the west end of the park, large clusters of children had gathered to wait for the puppet show, and Katie and Jody begged to be allowed to join them.

"I have to admit, this really *is* something," Mase said as they watched the children enjoying themselves. "I can't believe how many people are here. I was stationed near here for several years, and I'd never even heard of this."

"It took a while for our festivals to catch on, but they're getting more popular every year. We started out with the May Fest, then the Autumn Leaf Festival. Christmas Lighting is the newest, and the most popular. The hotels are booked for festival weekends a year in advance. That's one of the reasons why I think it's a shame no one has given that ski lodge another try.''

A few minutes later, Katie and Jody rejoined them, and little Jeremy began to fuss and cry. Evie glanced at her watch and saw that it was lunchtime.

''Who's hungry?'' she asked.

''Me,'' the twins yelled in unison.

''Me,'' Mase breathed into her ear. The look in his eyes told her that his hunger was not for food.

Evie sighed with relief when Mase lifted the baby out of the carrier and removed it from her shoulders. After taking off her own coat, she freed Jeremy from his bulky snowsuit. She balanced him expertly on her hip as she dug through the huge bag that Susan had left for him.

A few minutes later they sat in a circle around Evie's dining room table, munching happily on sandwiches with potato chips and large glasses of milk. Evie alternated eating bites of her own lunch with spooning pureed beef and noodles into Jeremy's appreciative mouth.

Mase watched her snuggle the boy on her lap, his head resting against the softness of her rounded breasts. For a brief moment he imagined that they were a family. A warm feeling of contentment washed over him.

He surprised himself with feelings he hadn't

known existed. For the first time he realized how much he had missed the warmth and belonging that came with a loving family.

What would it be like, he wondered, to come home to a family like this at the end of every day? It was a kind of security he had missed during his youth and had never expected to know.

"Can we go back now?" Jody asked thickly after stuffing the last half of his sandwich into his mouth. "I wanna see 'em build the snowmen."

"I suppose so, if everybody's finished," Evie agreed. "But I have to change the baby first. I hate to take him back out. He should be taking his nap."

"Isn't there someone who could watch him for you?" Mase inquired.

"Maybe I could leave him downstairs with Liesel. I'll ask her after I change his diaper."

The snowman contest was well under way when they had finally settled Jeremy's portable crib in Evie's office, where Liesel and her helpers could keep a watchful eye on him. The center of town was so packed that they could hardly move, and Mase and Evie each kept a firm hold on the small hand that nestled in theirs.

By three o'clock, evening was already beginning to darken the winter sky. The snow, which had been threatening to fall all day, began to drift lazily to earth. The temperature took a sharp drop, and despite their warm clothing, Mase and Evie were soon chilled to the bone. The children were apparently too busy to notice the change.

Finally, as dusk completely blanketed the town,

all the lights in Leavenworth were turned off. All over town people stared at the darkened street, waiting for the moment of Christmas lighting.

As the clock sounded the hour, the lights came to blazing life. Every building, tree, and bush in town was outlined in twinkling red, blue, and green. Although she had seen it many times before, Evie's breath still caught in her throat as she stared in wonder at the sight.

Mase's arm encircled Evie's shoulders and he hugged her to him. Everyone stood for a long moment before gathering their things together and fanning out away from the center of town. Even the usually talkative twins were silent as they made their way over to the restaurant to reclaim little Jeremy.

Evie found that his baby-sitters were most reluctant to part with him. Liesel picked him up as Mase folded up his crib.

"I always vanted to have children," she told Evie quietly. "But my husband died before we had been blessed, and I didn't find another man I vanted to try with while I was young enough."

Her eyes rested lovingly on Ben, and they said more than any words could utter. Love. It was a strange thing. You could look for it all your life, and then, just when you least expected it, it would drop right on top of you.

"Now it is too late," Liesel said sadly.

"No, Liesel," Evie said with certainty. "It's never too late for love."

She took Jeremy into her arms and followed

Mase up the stairs. Liesel watched her, her eyes glowing with a new understanding.

"At last," she murmured to herself, "Evie is no longer a stranger to love."

ELEVEN

Mase was busy building a fire in the fireplace when Evie joined him in her apartment. She helped the tired children strip off their wet coats and boots before taking off her own.

She went to put Jeremy to bed, and when she came back, Mase was waiting for her.

"Where are the twins?" he asked.

"I made a deal with them. There's a Christmas special they want to see on television tonight so they're taking a nap until dinner is ready."

"When *will* dinner be ready?"

"In about an hour. I'm going to fry chicken."

"That should give me plenty of time," he said with satisfaction.

"Time for what?"

"To take a shower, of course. I didn't get to take an hour-long bath this morning like some people."

While Mase was busy with his shower, Evie got a package of chicken out of the freezer and put it in the microwave to defrost. The chicken was sizzling on the stove and Evie had just started to wash the dishes when he snuck up behind her, wrapping his arms around her and pulling her back against his damp, bare chest.

He smelled very good to her, like soap, minty toothpaste, and warm, aroused man. His hand cupped a breast, and when he squeezed it lightly, the memory of his hands caressing her naked flesh burned through her.

His warm lips nibbled teasingly at the sensitive cords of her neck, and the arousal she had sensed began to press hot and hard against her jeans-clad bottom. He was wearing nothing but a rather threadbare towel wrapped around his middle, she realized with a start.

"Feeling tired, honey?" he asked with seductive intent. "I think we deserve a little 'nap,' too."

His hot, wet tongue caressed the shell of her ear, and when he breathed into it, a shiver of pleasure rippled through her. Pleased with his strategy, he tried to slip his hand down the front of her jeans, and got a faceful of soapsuds for his trouble.

"You nut," she said in exasperated amusement. "Don't you know the kids could walk out here at any moment? Go get dressed."

When dinner was finished, Mase watched television with Katie and Jody while Evie gave Jeremy his bath. By the time she had put the baby down for the night, Mase had learned more about the origins of Santa Claus and his reindeer than he had ever wanted to know.

"Come on, kids," Evie called. "Time for bed."

"Aw, can't we stay up a little longer, Aunt Evie?" Jody cajoled.

"No way. Our agreement was that you got to stay up for the Christmas special, and it's over now. Into bed."

"They're great kids," Mase said after watching Evie tuck them into bed. A hint of a smile lurked on his lips. "But like I said, I've never really been around kids much before. Today was an education."

"They *are* great, aren't they? Someday I'd like . . ."

"What would you like, Evie?"

"Never mind." She turned away from him.

"Someday you'd like to have a house full of kids just like them, wouldn't you?" he answered for her. "Why are you afraid to say it? Right now it sounds like a terrific idea."

"Sure," she said sadly. "Right now it does. I think you'd better go now, Mase."

"Why? And don't try to tell me you don't want to make love with me tonight, honey, because you know I can prove you're lying."

"I *can't* make love with you tonight. Not with the children here. I just wouldn't feel right. Please don't push me about this, Mase. I know as well as you do that you could get me to change my mind, but please don't try."

"Okay, honey. You've got a reprieve for tonight, but I'll be back in the morning. I want to take all of you out to my cabin for breakfast.''

Their parting kiss was passionately, infinitely sweet. It would have to keep both of them warm through the long, lonely night.

TWELVE

True to his word, Mase was back early the next morning. The children were delighted to ride in his battered old truck. It was an adventure to them, as was their visit to the strange house deep in the forest.

Evie stepped from the entryway into a spacious living room with a vaulted ceiling and a huge, dramatic black stone fireplace. The cabin was much larger than she had expected. The long wall along the back was made entirely of glass, giving them a panoramic view of the surrounding countryside.

"Go ahead and look around," Mase invited. "The kids are going to help me fix breakfast, aren't you, kids?"

He took Jeremy from her, heading toward the back of the cabin, where she assumed the kitchen must be. Jody and Katie trailed after him, leaving Evie alone in the immense room that was something out of a decorator's magazine.

Was this how Mase was accustomed to living?

she wondered. Her heart sank down to her feet. She stepped down the hall to peer into the master bedroom. It was as large as her entire apartment.

Consistent with the grand scale of the room, the black lacquer-framed bed was the largest Evie had ever seen. It was covered by a bedspread printed in a unique geometrical design, using varied shades ranging from pale mauve to deep violet.

The pièce de resistance was a raised platform in the corner of the room, with a round, black marble Jacuzzi. This must have been the tub which Mase had talked about. It could seat at least two people.

"What do you think of it?" Mase asked from the doorway.

"It's kind of overwhelming."

"That's a kind way to put it. It's easy to see what the friend who loaned it to me used this place for. I'd say it's definitely *not* for vacations with his wife and teenage kids."

Mase looked wonderfully out of place in this oppressively elegant room, wearing his faded jeans and ragged old sweatshirt, she thought. Evie walked over to him, wrapping her arms around his waist and hugging him tightly. His arms came around her, returning the hug in full measure.

"You don't like it here, either, do you?" she asked.

"I won't say it wouldn't be fun for a vacation with the right person," he replied with a sexy little grin. "But if you mean would I like to live here, then I'd have to say no. My taste doesn't run to anything quite this fancy."

"I'm glad," she replied with a tremulous smile.

They ignored the overly elegant dining room and breakfasted on delicious blueberry pancakes and bacon in the kitchen. After cleaning up the dishes, they all went outside to build a snowman.

By noon they were exhausted and half frozen. They went inside to warm up before driving back to town. The children's parents would be home soon, and Evie wanted to be at her apartment to meet them.

Mase was surprised at his reluctance to see their little interlude end. He had enjoyed the time he'd spent with the children, and Evie's small apartment seemed very empty without them. Still, there was one undeniable benefit to being alone with her, and he intended to make the most of it.

Evie had gone into the bathroom to change her clothes a few minutes earlier, just after her cousins had picked up their children. Did she have another surprise like that sexy blue underwear awaiting him? The thought made his blood run hot.

When she rejoined him a few minutes later, he was disappointed to find that she was covered from head to toe in an unprovocative costume of jeans and a heavy, bulky knit sweater. Oh well, he would soon take care of that.

"I'm sorry, Mase. I have a lot of work downstairs that I have to take care of," she apologized, dashing his hopes of a passion-filled afternoon. "I haven't been paying enough attention to my business lately."

"That's all right, honey," he said, hiding his

disappointment. "I can wait until tonight if I have to."

"Uhh, that's another thing," she hedged. "You see, I'm going to be busy tonight, too."

"Busy with what?"

"I have choir practice at church. We could have dinner at the restaurant before I go if you'd like."

"Only if I can go with you tonight and listen."

"You don't really want to go, do you, Mase? It'll be so boring for you."

"Impossible. I'm never bored when I'm with you."

Mase proved to be right. After sharing Liesel's fabulous sauerbraten, they walked to the rustic little church at the edge of town.

He sat in the back pew, not wanting to distract Evie or attract unwanted attention from other members of the choir. He listened with interest as they sang the scales to warm up their voices and tried to focus in on her voice alone, but like a truly good choir, their voices blended into one. It was not until Evie rose to sing her solo that Mase realized that with her clear, contralto voice she was very talented.

Her face grew reverent as she sang the sweet notes of "What Child Is This?" She lost herself in the music, not even noticing Mase's intent eyes as they watched her.

Could this dark-haired angel really be the woman who had made such passionate love with him just two nights ago, he asked himself, that wanton seductress in silk stockings and blue lace who had been constantly in his thoughts since the moment he had met her?

For all her inexperience, Mase had never known a more responsive or passionate lover, but there was so much more to Evie than that.

He wanted to know everything about her life, the things that had made her what she was today. And more than anything else, he wanted to know what had happened to make her so afraid of men that she had remained a virgin, emotionally at least, until she had met him.

Mase was so lost in his thoughts that he was not aware that the singers had finished their practice until he discovered Evie standing beside him. She smiled at him ruefully.

"I knew you'd be bored."

"Bored? No way," he assured her, rising to his feet and cupping her cheek in his large hand. "It's been an interesting evening, but I'm ready to go home now."

"That sounds good to me," she replied. The glowing look in her eyes was both his answer and his reward. "Let's go."

They walked hand in hand, their gloved fingers entwined, as they headed toward home. The simple fact that Mase would call her apartment "home" filled Evie with a warmth that stayed with her all through their long, cold walk.

The apartment had stood empty almost all day, and a damp cold permeated the air. After taking off her coat, she shivered, hugging her arms to her chest.

"Maybe we should start a fire," she suggested.

"I don't think we need to bother," he replied.

"Uh . . . would you like a drink?"

"No thanks." He hid a smile, touched by her awkward manner.

"Can I hang up your coat for you?"

"Thank you," he said politely, waiting for her to complete the task. "Now it's my turn."

"What do you mean?" she asked, retreating instinctively as he advanced on her.

"It's not that I didn't enjoy being seduced the other night," he assured her as she backed nervously into the breakfast bar. "It's just that I've been fantasizing about undressing you and carrying you off to bed since the first time I saw you."

He tugged the heavy sweater over her head and tossed it casually on to a chair before she knew what had happened. His deft fingers unhooked her bra, and as he peeled it away, her breasts tumbled free of their confines. The bra followed the path of her sweater.

"Mase, please . . ." she protested half-heartedly.

"Please what?" he inquired, his eyes rising from those coral-tipped mounds to look into her eyes.

A deep flush traveled from her cheekbones down to the beginning swell of the breasts which ached for his touch. The piercing heat of his gaze made her shiver. She wondered if she would ever grow accustomed to standing naked before a man after Allen . . .

"You're blushing again," he observed with satisfaction. "And just after you'd managed to convince me the other night that you were a shameless hussy. Please what, Evie? Please touch you?'' His fingers brushed lightly across her swollen nipples, and she shivered anew. ''Please kiss you?'' His hands captured hers and pressed them down on the bar behind her.

When his mouth claimed hers, their hands were the only other parts of their bodies that touched, but it was enough to send them both into a frenzy of need. He released her hands and knelt to unfasten her jeans and slip them off, taking her panties with them. She was even more beautiful than he'd remembered.

Mase guided her down the hall and into her bedroom. It was as different from the elegant boudoirs in which women usually entertained him as it could possibly be. He urged Evie down on the ruffled lavender comforter without speaking, and touched it with a respect that bordered on awe. This room was like the woman before him, simply and uncomplicatedly feminine.

The bed dipped as Mase sat down beside her on the edge, careful not to touch her. Evie felt completely vulnerable lying naked under his searing gaze while he was still fully dressed. She wished he would do something, say something to clear the tension from the air.

''Mase, you're making me very uncomfortable. I feel a little underdressed.''

''Don't ever be embarrassed with me, Evie. Your body is so beautiful. I love to see you this way. You don't know what it does to me to have you naked and trembling, waiting for the touch of my hands. You feel vulnerable now, and that bothers you, doesn't it? Yes, I can see that it does. Hasn't it occurred to you yet that even though I'm fully dressed, I'm just as vulnerable to *you* as you are to me?''

Wide, uncertain gray eyes stared up at Mase. She wanted desperately to believe what he was saying.

''Maybe I'll just have to prove it to you,'' he said.

With a quick motion he drew his own sweater over his head and gave it a toss. He stood, and his jeans and shorts followed, leaving him as magnificently bare to her eyes as she was to his.

When he joined her on the bed, they both rolled on to their sides and lay there, so close that each could feel the other's breath on their faces.

Evie's hand touched his chest tentatively. Mase went still, fearful of frightening her away.

It was the first time Evie had really allowed herself to look at his body. His broad shoulders, hard biceps, and forearms bespoke tremendous strength. Crisp dark hair covered his muscular chest, and her hand followed its shadowy trail down his flat belly and beyond. She realized gratefully that Mase's body was nothing like Allen's.

''That's right, Evie,'' he encouraged. ''Touch me, please. Don't be afraid, it's just another part of my body. A part that's very familiar with *your* body's secrets. It's your turn to learn about mine.''

She hesitated for just a moment, and then her hand reached down to cup him. Her first reaction was surprise at his softness. Growing bolder, her hand began to stroke ever so slightly. Mase moaned and shivered, his body going taut under that timid caress.

He swelled and grew harder, the silk now covering steel. Another tremor shook him, and Evie marveled at her ability to arouse him. And there was no mistaking the fact that he *was* aroused.

When she leaned forward to brush her lips across his, Mase seized her mouth, his tongue spearing between her lips in imitation of the act his body craved. It took supreme effort of will to keep from rolling her beneath him and taking what he needed.

As her free hand boldly explored his body, he thought he was going out of his mind. His hands clutched desperately at the comforter, his knuckles turning white with the effort.

Evie's hands roamed over his body, growing more and more assured with each passing moment. A low moan escaped his clenched jaw. A heady feeling of feminine power washed over her as he trembled under her touch.

"Honey, please," he pleaded. "I'm a flesh and blood man, not a piece of stone. I'll hold out as long as I can, but there are limits. Push me too far, and you'll find out what they are."

Evie was nearly as breathless as Mase, her body trembling with desire. She had learned her next lesson. It seemed that passion was a two-edged sword.

"Maybe I'm trying to push you past those limits," she said provocatively, her hand moving against his hot, painfully engorged manhood.

"Then take what you want."

"What?" she faltered, her newfound courage deserting her.

"It's all right. Come here, and I'll show you how," Mase encouraged.

He wrapped his arms around her and rolled her on top of him, guiding her shapely thighs downward so that she straddled his hips. Her long, unbound hair fell around them like a silken veil, shutting out the rest of the world.

Mase soothed her with soft words of reassurance, pressing kisses over any part of her anatomy within his reach. He did not want to undermine her control over this encounter, but at the same time he struggled to keep her arousal at the same fever pitch as his own.

She sensed instinctively what he wanted her to do, and her fingers found him once again. He drew in a sharp breath, and his body went rigid. Plump, rosy-tipped breasts swayed sensuously in front of him, and Mase could not resist cupping their fullness. He urged her torso down until he could catch her in his mouth.

A delicate shudder rippled through Evie's body and her hand tightened convulsively around him.

"Yes, Evie," he groaned. "That's right, love. Take me into you."

It was all the encouragement she needed. Her hand guided him to the threshold of her softness, pausing for a brief moment before lowering herself onto him.

She gasped, clutching at his sweat-dampened shoulders to steady herself. The sensations she was experiencing were incredibly intense.

His hands were all over her body. He caressed and tormented every soft, sensitive spot until she trembled with a need she had never dreamed she could experience.

Release came quickly, rocking them with the intensity of an earthquake. Evie collapsed on his broad chest and lay there, gasping for breath.

Mase's arms held her to him, stroking the long, smooth line of her back. She smiled to herself, pressing soft kisses over his chest and neck. She had never felt so completely contented before in her life.

"I suppose we should climb under the covers," she suggested, snuggling against him. "It's cold in here. You didn't give me a chance to turn on the heat."

"I'm warm enough," he replied, his voice lazy with satisfaction.

"You would be," she grumbled good-naturedly. "You're using *me* for your blanket."

"You might have spoiled me for life, you know. I'll never be satisfied with wool again."

"Very funny. It's easy for you to joke. You're not the one whose rear end is freezing."

"We can't let that happen, now can we?" His hands moved downward to the roundness of her bottom.

Evie sighed with pleasure as he stroked and caressed the cold flesh with his warm hands. Her skin heated instantly under his expert hands.

Affected just as much as she, his manhood stirred within her once again.

"Mase . . ." she protested, her hands reaching behind her to swat at his.

"I'm only trying to stimulate your circulation," he lied unconvincingly.

"That's not all you're trying to stimulate," she accused.

His hips rotated against hers, and Evie's breath grew labored. She could feel him grow hard deep inside her. A sense of wonder swept over her, and she marveled at the sensations which Mase so easily evoked.

"Can you pull rabbits out of hats, too?" she asked him, her voice deepening with desire.

"What do you mean?" he asked in confusion.

"I just wondered what other magic tricks you know. Or does your magic only work on me?"

His arms tightened around her and he rolled her over on her back, supporting himself on his elbows. He looked down into her softly sensual gray eyes, and suddenly he knew what she meant.

"It only works *in* you, my love," he said, starting to stroke deeply in and out. "Only in you."

Evie awoke very early the next morning. For a few minutes she simply lay there beside Mase, reveling in a closeness she had never known with another human being. She knew she would never know it with anyone else. Only Mase. Her magic man.

Although she was reluctant to leave the warm comfort of her shared bed, Evie wanted to surprise

Mase with an elegant breakfast of *her* making, rather than his. Slowly, with great care, she slipped out of his arms and into the icy embrace of the cold morning air. She dashed to the heat control beside the door and turned it up.

Evie longed for the comfort of her warm, fuzzy pink bathrobe, but she refused to allow Mase to see her in that prosaic creation. Gritting her teeth against the icy cold, she donned the sexy beige lace nightie and robe that had been her other purchases at the infamous Love Boutique.

After slipping her feet into frivolous little slippers, she stepped out into the living room, closing the door securely behind her. She turned up the heat in the front of the apartment, too, before starting breakfast.

She was breaking eggs into a bowl when a knock sounded on her front door. Evie hurried to answer it, not wanting the noise to awaken Mase.

When she opened the door and peeked through the crack, her face turned deathly white and a strange ringing sounded in her ears. The nightmare had come to her again with a vengeance, but this time she was wide-awake.

THIRTEEN

"Well, what kind of greeting is this for your long lost daddy, Evie girl?"

The tall, bulky man pushed the door open, and Evie was too stunned to try to stop him. As his eyes took in her revealing costume, she longed to cover herself from his gaze.

"Haven't you got a kiss for your old man after all these years?"

"You're not my father," she bit out. "Why have you come here? What do you want from me?"

"Best I can tell, you don't have anything worth taking," he said, his eyes traveling contemptuously around the modest room.

"It was *you*," she accused, her eyes flashing silver fire. Studying the mocking expression on his face, Evie was certain that Kyle had been the one who'd been in her apartment that night, as well as the one who'd vandalized her restaurant.

"I don't know what you're talking about," he denied.

"You know exactly what I'm talking about," she shot back, angry sparks shooting from her eyes. "You broke into my apartment, and you tried to ruin my restaurant. Why didn't you trash my apartment too?

"We interrupted you, didn't we," she went on, answering her own question. "You must have thought Mase was coming in with me. You wouldn't have run off just because of me.

"Why, Kyle? Were you using the vandalism to cover up something else? Just what were you looking for, anyway?"

"Maybe I came for what should have been mine all along," he growled menacingly. "Your father had money when he died. If I hadn't been sure of that, I'd never have married your ma. All these years, I just figured I'd been wrong. Then Marge finally admitted the truth. She told me he'd left it in a trust for you. I came here to get what's due me."

"Get what's due you for what?" Evie flared. "For destroying my family and abusing my mother for over twenty years?"

"You always did have a sharp tongue," he said. Only his eyes betrayed his anger. "Most men shy away from a woman like that. It's a shame you didn't take after your mother in that respect. At least she knew how to keep her mouth shut."

"Oh, yes," she replied bitterly. "You taught her that lesson the first time you broke her jaw."

"Why, you little bitch," he sputtered. "Maybe it's time to teach *you* that lesson, too."

Kyle took a step toward her, and Evie's eyes

grew wide. Fear held her motionless, like a rabbit caught in a trap. His arm drew back and she waited for the blow to fall.

"Evie?" Mase's deep, familiar voice reached out to her from the door of the bedroom. It was as if she had been drowning and he had thrown her a lifeline. "Is everything all right?"

She wheeled toward him and Mase took in every detail of her tense body and frightened face. His long legs took him to her side in a few strides and his brawny arm encircled her protectively, holding her slightness firmly against his bare chest and jeans-clad legs.

"Evie? What's going on?"

"Richards is the name," he blustered. "But my friends call me Kyle. I'm Evie's stepfather."

"What can we do for you, *Mr. Richards*," he inquired, the not-so-subtle nuance in his voice warning the man to watch his step.

"I'm just back from spending six years in South America. I made a special trip up here to give Evie some news in person," he paused.

"What news?" she questioned, her courage bolstered by Mase's presence.

"About your ma. I'm afraid she had a little accident. Fell and broke her neck about a month ago. Killed her, it did."

Tears stung her eyes, but she blinked them back furiously. She would not give this man the satisfaction of seeing her pain.

Evie remembered how many times Kyle had caused her mother to have "accidents." She swallowed the bile that was rising up in her throat.

Anger burned hotly within her, driving out the shock-induced numbness. Evie stiffened and pulled herself out of Mase's arms. For once she faced her stepfather and stared him down.

"Get out of here, Kyle."

"So this is the thanks I get for going out of my way to break the news to you myself," he exploded. "I don't know why I expected anything else. I should have taught you some respect when you were still a kid. I would have, too, if it hadn't been for your ma."

Evie stared at her stepfather with cool deliberation. She would show him that she was no longer the frightened, timid child he had once tyrannized.

"Show respect for what?" she questioned contemptuously. "Get out. Get out of my house and don't ever come back."

Her spine remained stiff as a board as she watched him turn and leave, though Mase could see the effort it cost her. She stood there for a long time, staring at the closed door until he stepped behind her and wrapped his strong arms around her.

Those arms had never seemed more comforting or more supportive. She turned gratefully and buried her face in his shoulder.

Mase drew her over to the big, overstuffed chair and cuddled her on his lap. She clung tightly to him as the tears, which she had managed to hold back in front of Kyle, finally overwhelmed her.

The depth of her grief was genuine, but buried deep beneath it was an uneasy blend of anger and guilt. Anger at her mother for allowing Kyle to terrorize them both and tear their family apart, and guilt for her own ultimate inability to save her mother from her stepfather's brutality.

In the days that followed, Mase and Evie continued to spend as much time together as her schedule would allow, but their relationship had undergone a subtle change.

Evie withdrew into herself. She had been badly upset by the appearance of her stepfather after so many years. How grateful she had been for Mase's presence that morning, more grateful than she had ever been for anything in her life.

She waited anxiously for Kyle to approach her again, but to her surprise, he seemed to have vanished. Evie found it difficult to believe that she had rid herself of him so easily.

She realized that she was reverting to the defensive behavior of her childhood, but she could not help herself. A bitter smile curved her lips but did not reach her eyes. The closeness that she had sensed between Mase and herself that morning of Kyle's unexpected visit had died in an instant.

After all these years she had forgotten the cardinal rule. Evie had allowed someone to get too close. Deep down inside, she was still that same frightened child who had arrived in Leavenworth so many years ago, just as alone, and just as hungry for love.

Her gray eyes were empty when she looked up from her desk to stare at the clock on the wall of her tiny office. It was getting late. Soon Mase would arrive to take her out for the evening.

During the past week he had shared dinner with her at the restaurant every night, keeping her company through the long hours of the evening.

It was the most exquisite misery Evie had ever experienced. To be in Mase's arms, their bodies as close as it was humanly possible for them to be, but having to hold her emotions under tight control.

Although she was sure it was unintentional, Mase was making it harder than it needed to be. He was being so gentle, his strong arms so protective, his hands and lips tender, almost loving.

Evie longed with every fiber of her being to surrender to that gentleness. She wanted to tell him the story of her childhood and the painful experience of her brief engagement to Allen.

From her early childhood, Evie had dreamed of finding someone in whom she could confide. Someone to whom she could reveal the painful memories that she had hidden away for so long. She sensed that in sharing those secrets she would somehow free herself from the past.

For a brief time she had allowed herself to hope that Mase would be that someone, but now, at last, she faced the truth. The memories, and more importantly the guilt, had been hidden deep within her for so long that she had built a protective wall around them. She doubted if anyone, even Mase, could break through it now. Why not simply give up? she asked herself in despair.

Each day Evie told herself that she would put an end to the torment that night. Then, when she saw Mase again, she did not have the strength to

send him away. All too soon their time together
would end. The thought of a lifetime of lonely
nights spent in a cold, empty bed would send her
running back into his arms.

A heavy sigh escaped her lips and she ran her
slender fingers through tousled curls. It was past
time to go upstairs and change. The restaurant was
closed that night, and Mase had made mysterious
plans for them. He would tell her nothing, except
that she needed to wear her warmest clothes.

Anyway, it was useless to torture herself this
way. She reluctantly admitted the truth to herself.
This time with Mase was just too precious to lose.
Ending her affair with him was simply beyond her
capability.

Mase walked slowly down the deserted road,
trying to figure a way out of his dilemma. For the
first time since he was a boy, he was involved in
a situation that he could not control. He did not
like the feeling.

At least he had been able to deal quickly and
effectively with Kyle Richards. It had been hours
before Evie's initial grief had eased to the point
where he could leave her alone. Once he'd accomplished that, Mase had set out in search of him.

The older man had not been hard to find. The
only tavern in town had just opened for the day.
Mase found him alone at the bar, and the drink
he was tossing down was obviously not the first
he had indulged in that day.

A reminiscent smile crossed Mase's face. It was
just as well that Evie was not there to see it, he

recognized, for it was filled with a primitive, masculine satisfaction that would have made her very nervous indeed.

Mase was well aware that he could be intimidating on occasion, and he had utilized that ability to its fullest extent in his encounter with Kyle Richards. He did not think the older man would ever dare to come near her again.

The fear on Evie's face when he found her with Richards had filled him with a possessive fury that had startled him. Until her stepfather had appeared on her doorstep, Mase had not realized the depth of his feelings for her. He had been content to let their relationship slide comfortably along, taking their easy companionship for granted. Then, suddenly it was gone.

Relationships with women had always come easily to him. Granted, they had been only physical relationships, but until he'd met Evie, that was all he had wanted. For the first time he was being forced to pursue the woman of his choice, and the more determined his pursuit grew, the more elusive Evie became.

Patience was not a part of his nature, and at times he had chafed at the effort it took, but so far he had managed to be unfailingly kind and gentle with her, taking care to conceal the intensity of his emotions. He tried to remember what a shock the news of her mother's death must have been to her.

What could he do if she continued to act this way, though? He could not force her to confide in

him, any more than he could force her to love
him.

Love? Where had that thought come from? Did
he truly want Evie to love him?

The only time he seemed to be able to break
through her steel wall of reserve was in bed. Her
physical responsiveness gratified him in a way, but
he wanted her to need him for more than simple
stud service. He wanted to batter down her
defenses and force her to involve him in all aspects
of her life.

She had been working very hard lately, trying
to take care of her business and still spend time
with him. Perhaps a night out to relax and simply
have fun would help. If not, he would have to
take more drastic measures.

He shook his head as he mounted the stairway
to her apartment. Mase just wished he knew what
those measures would be.

It had been many years since Evie had gone on
a sleigh ride. When she was in school, large
groups of her friends used to have sleighing parties
during the holidays, but since she had gotten
older, most of those friends had moved away.

Making friends had always been difficult for
Evie. Since she had come back to town to start her
restaurant, she found that she knew many people
casually, but there were few who she knew intimately enough to call by that title.

Susan and Jenny were her cousins, but did that
necessarily make them her friends? She thought
not. Friendship was something that had to be

earned. Liesel? She had confided more in her cook than she had in her family, but the woman was too conscious of being Evie's employee for their relationship to go that final step.

Ironically, if Evie were asked to name her best friend, her answer could only be Mason Kincaid. She had shared more of herself with him, felt more at ease with him, and cared more for him than anyone else she knew. When he left, as he surely would, she would lose both her lover and her friend in one swift stroke. A shaft of pain cut through her, leaving her with an empty ache inside.

Mase climbed into the back of the huge, hay-filled sleigh, bending down to help her up. She watched him as he picked a comfortable spot in a corner, studying his familiar features in the moonlight.

Nothing Mase did was casual. Everything from eating to making love was done with an intensity that was characteristic of him.

"Hey," he called to her. "Are you going to stand there all night?"

She looked down to find him seated comfortably with his back resting against the side of the sleigh and his knees bent, his arms resting on them. He patted the spot in front of him invitingly.

She sat down between his strong thighs, unfolding her blanket and draping it around them. There was a large group in spite of the cold, she thought, looking at the others who would share their ride.

"Uh uh," Mase said, his hands going around her to unbutton her coat. "Take this off first."

"Are you crazy? I'll freeze to death."

"No you won't," he denied, stubbornly inching her coat off her arms.

When he pulled her back against his broad, hard chest, his own coat was open, and she could feel the steady, comforting heat of his body pressed to hers. Maybe he wasn't crazy after all.

Mase draped her coat across her chest and wrapped them both in the blanket. He crossed his arms over her and Evie nestled back, her aching loneliness of a moment past, gone as if by magic.

The night was bitterly cold, and the moonlight reflected brilliantly on the soft white snow. Above them, stars twinkled like sparkling drops of ice on a canopy of black velvet. Gaily colored Christmas lights adorned the sleigh and the driver's seat, illuminated it seemed, by magic alone.

The sleigh gave a lurch before beginning its smooth, gliding trip across the crusty whiteness. The silence surrounded them, broken only by the scrape of the runners on the snow, the rhythmic clip-clop of the horses' hooves on the frozen ground, and the crystalline tinkling of the sleigh bells.

The frigid air soon brought a rosy pinkness to any skin it touched. Evie huddled deeper under the warmth of their blanket.

"Come on, folks," the driver jibed good-naturedly. "It doesn't sound very jolly back there. Let's sing some carols."

He started them out with a robust version of "Jingle Bells." By the time they were halfway through "Deck the Halls," he no longer found it necessary to keep things going. The entire group was singing with gusto.

Beneath the heavy cover of the blanket, their bodies huddled closer together, communicating in a way that made words unnecessary. A cloud obscured the moonlight, and Evie looked back over her shoulder, her cheek rubbing along the smoothness of Mase's throat. His lips sought hers, stealing lingering kisses that were somehow more exciting because of their secrecy.

She could feel passion rising within her, but for the first time, it was not a mindless need that demanded immediate gratification. It was a warmer, softer thing that was more than mere physical desire.

Mase's arms tightened around her, and suddenly she knew that he was experiencing the same sensations. Her hand moved to his, and he caught it in his strong clasp. Evie wished vainly that the ride would never end.

On the trip back to town in Mase's pickup, Evie sat just as close to him as she could get. Her hand rested intimately on his jeans-clad thigh, provocatively massaging the hard muscles.

The trip seemed to last forever. When Mase finally brought his truck to a stop on the small road behind the restaurant, they hurried silently up the stairs like two children playing a secret game.

An eternity later, their passion spent, their bodies lay entwined in the middle of Evie's bed. The room was cold, but under the old down-filled quilt, they were deliciously warm.

She was at peace with herself for the first time

in days as she listened to the satisfying sound of her lover's breathing. A smile rested easily on her lips as she joined him in slumber.

Unbidden and unexpected, like a thief in the night, the nightmare came.

FOURTEEN

Her surroundings were vague but oddly familiar. The moon shone brightly through the trees, illuminating the lush landscape and casting strange, sinister shadows on the uneven ground.

The taste of fear was acrid on Evie's tongue as she sought a place to hide amidst the dense growth of foliage. The thundering sound of her heartbeat echoed in her ears, and she struggled to force it back so that she could listen for a noise that would indicate pursuit.

She knew he was out there waiting for her to emerge from hiding, but she could not stay where she was forever. Her mother was depending on her.

It was so cold. A shiver rippled through her body and she huddled lower, trying to absorb the damp warmth which emanated from the ground beneath her.

She had to get to the garage. If she had her bicycle, she could go to town and bring back help.

Reluctantly, she left her secure little haven and set out into the cold, dark night.

All at once, he was there. She tried to run, but he knocked her to the ground. Her knee twisted under her and she cried out at the pain.

Large hands gripped her shoulders and she fought wildly to escape. Pain rippled down her leg, the intensity of it inspiring her to fight all the harder. She couldn't let him stop her, she thought frantically. She just couldn't!

"Evie."

The deep, familiar voice finally penetrated the dense fog of her nightmare. She stopped her struggles and blinked several times to clear the mists of sleep from her eyes.

Mase's brawny frame was bent over hers, his face filled with concern. Seeing the recognition in her eyes, he relaxed his grip.

"Mase?" she whispered, as if she couldn't believe he was really there. "Oh, Mase."

She threw herself into his arms, trembling convulsively from the combination of cold and reaction. Her knee was twisted under his heavy leg, pain throbbed up her thigh into her hip, and a light film of perspiration covered her body.

He shifted off her leg, holding her tightly, and she surrendered to the comfort of his arms. Evie buried her face against his neck and wrapped her arms around his broad back.

After a moment, he eased over on his back, carrying her with him. He held her with one arm, using the other to pull the covers up over her quivering, naked body. He pressed soft, comforting kisses across her temple and cheek, one hand combing through her tangled curls.

"I'm sorry, Mase," she whispered at length. "I had a bad dream."

Mase wanted to question her about it, to find out why these dreams haunted her sleeping hours, but he knew that it was not the time to do it. He smiled in satisfaction as her tense body began to relax and the trembling subsided. One day soon he would know all there was to know about Evie's past.

_____ FIFTEEN _____

In the days that followed, Evie finally started to throw off the veil of shock which had surrounded her since she'd heard the news of her mother's death. The grief she had felt had not truly been for the loss of her mother, whom she had hardly known, Evie realized. It had been for the relationship they had never had.

The last remnants of her old life seemed to fade slowly away. It was time to look ahead and build a new life for herself. Wasn't that what this season symbolized?

The day of Christmas Eve was upon them and even that important question took a backseat to the last-minute rush of holiday duties that Evie hurried to complete. With growing excitement, she shopped, wrapped presents, and baked the traditional mince pies that would be her contribution to the huge dinner at her aunt and uncle's house.

She and Mase were invited to stay there overnight so that they would be there early for the

Christmas morning festivities. Evie was glad to be leaving her apartment and her memories behind for even that short time.

Her suitcase was packed, and several huge shopping bags filled with presents were sitting beside the door when Mase arrived. Evie was dressed in gray wool slacks and a soft, deep red sweater. Glittering red poinsettia earrings adorned her ears, but they were outshone by her glowing eyes.

Her childlike excitement was endearing, and Mase could not help an amused but affectionate smile. His eyes widened a bit as they took in the huge pile of boxes and sacks waiting to be carried down to the truck.

"I think maybe we'd better take your car tonight. I don't suppose you want any of this stuff to sit in the back of my pickup, and if we put it in the front, there wouldn't be room for us."

The same thing nearly held true in Evie's little car. Both the trunk and the backseat were filled to capacity, and she wound up holding the tray of pies on her lap while Mase maneuvered his long, muscular frame behind the wheel. After a brief struggle to get the seat pushed as far back as it would go, they were ready to leave.

Snow had begun to fall several hours before, and the huge white flakes floated silently to earth, assuring them of an old-fashioned white Christmas. The road was still relatively clear and the driving was easy as they headed back up the same highway they had traversed two short weeks before as strangers. Evie marveled at how much her life had changed in those weeks.

The companionable silence in the car was broken only by the staticky sound of distant Christmas music from the radio. Twilight was darkening into evening and occasionally the twinkling colors of Christmas lights could be seen along the roadside. A warm feeling of contentment filled Evie. All too soon, they entered the driveway heading to the house.

The house was warm and cozy, a fire blazing in the fireplace and the scent of roasting turkey filling the air. A huge fir tree sat in the place of honor in front of the living-room windows bearing its burden of glittery ornaments in patient majesty.

"Aunt Evie," Katie and Jody shrieked, running toward her.

She quickly set the pies down and knelt, opening her arms to receive the excited children. It was not a moment too soon.

"Sorry, Evie," a slender man of about Mase's age apologized with a laugh. "Hey, you little hooligans. Give your aunt Evie a chance to take her coat off.

"You must be Mase," he went on. "I'm Chad Marlow and this is Matt Freemont."

"You'll have to excuse this chaos," the other man said with a rueful smile. "It's the first year the kids have really been old enough to understand what's going on."

"It looks like I'm the last one to meet your friend, Evie" came a deep, rumbling voice from behind them.

"Hi, Uncle Jock," Evie greeted him with a smile. "Merry Christmas."

The tall, older man swept her into his arms and gave her a hug that took her breath away for a moment. When he released her, he looked the younger man over assessingly. His eyes were the same clear silvery gray as Evie's.

Seeming satisfied with what he saw, Jock held out his hand to Mase.

"Glad to meet you, son," he said. "I've been hearing about you from the girls. We're going to have to have a little talk."

"Now, Uncle Jock . . ." Evie started to protest.

"Hello, Evie. This must be the young man I've been hearing so much about," said a trim, older woman who had come up behind her.

"Where did you hear about him?" Evie asked, turning to her in surprise.

"Why, from the girls and Katie and Jody, not to mention half the people in town. Surely you've lived here long enough to know that nothing stays a secret for long."

"You're right, as always," Evie said with a soft laugh. "Aunt Janet, this is Mason Kincaid."

"How do you do, Mrs. Winthrop?" Mase said, taking her hand and holding it between both of his.

Her aunt was charmed and did not try to hide it. She smiled at him coyly, looking far younger than her years.

"Your taste in men is definitely improving," her aunt told her with at nod. "Hang on to this one, dear."

"I'll do my best to see that she does," Mase answered for her.

"Come along, Evie," Aunt Janet urged. "We need your help to get dinner ready."

Evie hesitated, realizing that despite his poise, Mase felt like a fish out of water in the midst of her family. Still, she couldn't stay with him every moment while they were there. Their eyes met and Evie shrugged helplessly, abandoning him to his fate.

By the time dinner was ready, Mase had joined the other men in several toasts, and he was filled with a warm, rosy glow. The abundance of food on the dining-room table stunned him. The aroma of the immense turkey with dressing, the honey-baked ham, and side dishes that he had never seen before in his life, filled the room, threatening to overload his senses. And the talking and laughter never seemed to stop.

Vague memories from his childhood tantalized him. Images of Christmas morning under the tree had been punctuated by the angry tones of his parents' fighting. Nothing had prepared him for a Christmas Eve celebrated with the boisterous exuberance of the Winthrop clan.

After the dinner dishes had been cleared away, they assembled in the living room. The children, already wearing red and white striped pajamas, hung their stockings by the mantel before being ushered up to bed.

The adults went to work in earnest, rescuing odd-shaped packages from their hiding places and wrapping them in gay red and green paper. The hours flew by, and soon it was time for the parents to wake their children.

The excited, sleepy-eyed tots tumbled down the stairway to sit, awed by the glorious sight of the tree which twinkled in the darkened room. Once the children had opened their presents from Santa, everyone hurried up to their rooms to change for the Christmas Eve services at church.

The rustic little church was beautiful, lit only by the tree and dozens of candles, and the service was correspondingly simple. The minister read the story of the first Christmas, and the congregation sang carols from shared hymnals.

When the service ended and they started for home, it was snowing lightly. The interior of the car was dark and very cozy, and Evie grew sleepy. As she sat in the circle of Mase's arms, her head drooped on his shoulder and she dozed comfortably. His arm tightened around her, holding her securely. A burst of cold air from the opening doors woke her abruptly, and she staggered out of the old station wagon.

They said their good nights in the hallway, Evie and Mase reluctantly going upstairs to their separate rooms at opposite ends of the house. Suddenly the sense of magic that had pervaded the evening was gone.

Evie absorbed the cold emptiness of the lonely bed, longing fervently for the touch of Mase's big body. She curled up in a ball, wrapping her heavy flannel nightgown around her, but it was no use.

The house was as still and silent as the snowy night when she stepped out into the hallway. Her bare feet carried her noiselessly across the wooden floor to Mase's door.

"Evie?" he breathed, instantly aware of her presence. He sat up to turn on the bedside lamp.

"I was lonesome," she explained in a whisper, lifting the edge of the covers to slip in with him.

"What if your family finds out?" he felt obliged to protest.

"I don't care. I just want to be with you."

She turned off the light and snuggled into his arms. The heat of his body penetrated the heavy layer of flannel between them, and she sighed contentedly.

They both knew that they would be overheard if they made love, but neither of them felt deprived as they lay entwined in each other's arms. Somehow just being together was enough. Moments later, they were asleep.

SIXTEEN

Evie rose with the dawn, hoping to slip back down to her own room unnoticed. She was just closing the door to Mase's room behind her when Susan and Matt emerged from the room next door. She struggled for composure in the face of their knowing looks.

"Are the children up already?" she asked.

"Not quite yet," Susan assured her. "We were just going down to plug in the tree lights before anyone else came down. Looks like you beat us though."

Several plausible excuses sprang to her lips, but Evie could not bring herself to utter them. She was not ashamed of her relationship with Mase.

"Go ahead and get things ready," she told her cousin. "Mase and I will be down in a few minutes."

Her cousin's mouth dropped as Evie all but confessed to her indiscretion.

"I didn't think she had it in her," Susan whispered to her husband as Evie disappeared down the hall.

The soft snowfall had apparently continued all through the night, and a good six inches had accumulated on the windowsill. A fire crackled cheerily on the hearth, dispelling the chill, and the huge tree glowed in the dim light of the early morning.

Mase sat quietly and studied Evie, his silence going unnoticed in the bustle of activities. She had never looked more beautiful than she did at that moment, he thought, loving the look of her hair all loose and slightly mussed and her face flushed with excitement.

As though aware of the intensity of his gaze, Evie looked at Mase, and against her will, a sudden blush rose up. The look in his eyes was more intimate than a kiss.

They opened their gifts amidst much laughter, interspersed with hugs and affectionate kisses. The children naturally stole the show, and Evie allowed herself to dream of the possibility of someday having little ones of her own. She had never admitted her desire to have children before, even to herself.

Mase exclaimed over the hand-knit sweater that Evie had found in a shop owned by an old friend. Evie was delighted with a blue silk blouse from her aunt and uncle and the pictures which Katie and Jody had drawn for her themselves, but she suddenly went quiet, her eyes wide with surprise as she opened Mase's gift.

"Oh, Mase," she said in hushed tones, lifting

the crystal castle music box out of its bed of tissue paper.

"Do you really like it?" he asked doubtfully.

"How can you even ask?" Her eyes spoke eloquently as they looked up into his face.

Once the gift exchange was over, they all helped to prepare an elegant brunch which was topped off by cups of hot, strong coffee with whipped cream and cinnamon.

After dressing, everyone pitched in to clean up the mess they had left from their orgy of gift opening. They roughhoused playfully, using balls of wadded-up wrapping paper for ammunition.

Mase chased Evie through the dining room, dodging around the table and chairs into the kitchen. She tried to slip behind the counter, but he caught her hand, jokingly twisting it up behind her back, while being careful not to hurt her.

Evie froze, her body tense with fear. The playful atmosphere was gone in an instant.

"Let me go, Mase," she said, her voice tight with tension. "Please, let me go."

He released her at once, shocked to see the fear and distrust in her face as she backed away from him. In a moment, she was gone.

Mase started to go after her, but Jock stepped out of the shadows and caught his arm.

"Leave her alone, Mase," he said, his hand stilling Mase's taut body. "I think we need to have that little talk now."

That evening Mase finally found himself alone in the big living room. Alone except for Jeremy.

He put the finishing touches on the fire which began to hiss and sputter, the flames shooting out around the dry, seasoned wood. When he turned, he found the enterprising tot trying to empty the contents of Evie's purse out on the floor.

"No you don't, sport," he scolded, picking the boy up in his arms and looking around helplessly. What did you do with a child this small, anyway?

Deprived of his objective and overtired from the busy day, Jeremy began to cry. Mase bounced him up and down in his arms in an effort to quiet him, but it only made him cry harder. Surrounded by adults who had never been eager to play, Jeremy had missed his nap. A cranky frown furrowed his little brow.

Mase looked around for help, a frantic expression on his face, but there was no help in sight. It was up to him to do something, but what?

He sat down on the couch in front of the fire and cradled the baby against his broad, hard chest. The crying ceased as if by magic.

Mase slouched down, and Jeremy lay there, his tiny chest rising and falling on that hard wall of muscle as if it were a feather bed. Little fists grasped handfuls of Mase's sweater. He yawned, burping slightly and going to sleep.

Mase stared down at the tiny blond head for a long time. Finally, a large, work-hardened hand gently caressed the silken baby curls, lifting them off the sleep-flushed face.

Evie watched them from the doorway for several minutes before he was aware of her presence. Tears stung her eyes and she blinked them away.

It was a side to Mase that she had never suspected was there. This was a man who would never willingly hurt a child, who would never, ever hurt her.

Their eyes met and held for a long moment before Evie turned and walked away.

They stayed to share a cold supper made from last night's leftovers. Evie was quiet and withdrawn, speaking only when directly addressed, and Mase's anger simmered beneath his cool exterior.

After loading almost as many packages back into Evie's car as they had come with, Mase climbed behind the wheel. Evie joined him, and they set off into the snowy night.

The snowfall had made the roads treacherous, and Mase had to concentrate all his efforts on driving. Evie stared out the window into the darkness, uncommunicative but apparently no longer afraid.

"Mase, that's my street there," she pointed out to him as they passed through town.

"I know," he replied shortly. "We're going to my place tonight."

"I'm really tired, Mase. I'd like to go home."

"No."

"What do you mean?"

"I mean no."

They sat in stony silence as the car continued through the countryside once again. The mood within its confines was anything but festive.

When they pulled up in front of the cabin, Mase

got out and carried their overnight bags in with him. Having no choice, Evie followed him.

"Just what does all this mean, Mase?" she asked. "I want to go home."

"You aren't leaving here until we get a few things settled."

"What things?"

"Nothing much. Just the fact that you seem to think I'm going to turn abusive, the way your stepfather did."

His words stunned Evie, and she stared at him with a blank look on her face. He eyed her with stony speculation.

"Who told you about that?" she asked. "Never mind. There's only one person who *could* have told you. Uncle Jock talks too much."

"Why did I have to hear it from him, Evie? I thought we were close. I thought you could tell me anything. Obviously I was wrong.

"You were afraid of me today," Mase said, his anger fading and the hurt showing in his voice. "That really hurt me. It also made me angry to think that you had so little faith in me. I suppose that by bringing you here, I was trying to prove that even though I was very angry, and even though *you* were alone and isolated with me here, I would never hurt you. Not all men are like your stepfather, Evie."

"Oh, Mase, don't you think I know that?" she replied, her soft lips trembling and her eyes misty with emotion. "You just caught me by surprise this afternoon. My reaction was instinctive. It doesn't mean I really thought you'd hurt me."

Long, dark lashes dropped to veil her vulnerable gray eyes, and Evie walked very willingly into his embrace. Strong arms encircled her shoulders, drawing her close. Evie sighed and rested her head on the reassuringly hard surface of Mase's chest.

"Kyle used to do that to my mother when he was angry," she explained in a soft voice. "Twist her arm, I mean. He broke her wrist once. He's a vicious man. He enjoys hurting people, and he always has to be in control. When I was growing up, he was like a puppeteer, and my mother and I were the toys that danced on the ends of his strings. I tried to fight him, but in the end I finally realized that I wasn't hurting anyone but my mother. You see, when he got angry with me, my mother always intervened. Then he got angry with *her* for sticking up for me, and he wound up taking it out on her. I swore that when I grew up, no man would ever do that to me. I can remember lying in bed at night when I was a little girl and hearing them in the next room. He hurt her. I don't know how and I don't want to know, but I'll never forget the sounds she would make, and how she would cry later. I think that in some twisted way, inflicting pain was what gave him his pleasure."

She fell silent, and Mase waited, studying her tormented face. He wished that there was something, anything, he could do to help her, but all he could do was listen.

"On my twelfth birthday, Mother baked a cake for me," she went on at last. "Kyle was late getting home, as usual, so we went ahead and had our party. When he got home, he flew into a drunken rage. He started to hit my mother.''

A series of uncontrollable tremors wracked her body and tears clogged her throat, making it hard for her to speak. Mase hugged her fiercely, trying to comfort her without interrupting the flow of words which had been locked up inside her for too long.

"He hurt her so badly. She was unconscious, but he just kept hitting her. I grabbed a lamp off a table and hit him over the head with it. I thought at first that I'd killed him, and I was glad. But I hadn't, and I couldn't, so I grabbed my coat and ran out the door. That's what my nightmare is about. He woke up and came after me. He caught me just as I was about to get my bike and ride to a friend's house for help. We struggled and he fell on top of me. That's when I hurt my knee, not in an accident. Some neighbors heard me screaming and called the police. I was in the hospital for several weeks. My knee was broken and the edge of the bone had cut the tendon, so I had to have surgery. Mother made me promise not to tell anybody what had happened.

"When I got out of the hospital she had my bags packed. She told me it wasn't safe for me to come home. I was so happy. I didn't understand what she was saying, you see. I thought we were *both* leaving, but she put me on a bus for Leavenworth and I never saw her again.''

Huge eyes, dark with pain, looked up into his. Shock held Mase silent. He tenderly brushed a long, tangled curl back from her face and tucked it behind her ear.

"Because of Kyle, I've never really trusted men. Even with Uncle Jock, it took a long time. I never even had a boyfriend until I was in college. Allen seemed to be the exact opposite from Kyle in every way. He was quiet and studious, and he abhorred violence of any kind. I was convinced that I'd finally found a man who was safe. I didn't realize until it was almost too late that there were other forms of abuse: subtle, but just as devastating. Allen told me that I was lucky I had him, because no other man would put up with me, and the worst part was that I started to believe him. Before I finally woke up and left him, he nearly destroyed what little confidence I had managed to develop."

"You really haven't had much luck with the men you've known, have you? I'm so sorry if I've hurt you, too."

"No, Mase. Don't ever think that," she denied vehemently. "Do you know that before I met you, I thought I was frigid? I felt like such a failure. When Allen and I had sex, I never felt anything but embarrassed and uncomfortable. I never dreamed I could feel the things I feel when I'm with you. After I ended my relationship with Allen, I was determined never to get involved with anyone again. Then I met you. I think I've known from the first that I could trust you. I just had to start believing it."

"Evie . . ." he said, his voice husky with emotion. "My sweet, darling Evie. I love you so much. I want to spend the rest of my life with you. I want to hold you and love you and protect you from the world. You belong to me now, just like I belong to you, and neither of us will ever be alone again.''

Evie wrapped her arms around his lean waist, and his arms surrounded her lovingly, crushing the softness of her breasts against the hardness of his chest. They made their way into the bedroom and finally knew the ultimate intimacy that comes with the joining of hearts and souls as well as bodies.

The next morning they were awakened from the blissful realms of slumber by the harsh, invasive ring of the telephone. Evie curled up in a ball, trying to absorb the warmth of the bed as she watched Mase talk on the phone at the other end of the room. She could not hear his words, but the tone of his voice troubled her. He glanced over at her, and she felt a chill of apprehension.

When he returned to sit beside her on the bed, Evie knew something was wrong. She watched him anxiously as he smoothed the blanket over her hip.

''Evie, I'm going to have to leave for a little while.''

''Where are you going?'' she asked in confusion.

''Seattle. There's something I have to do.''

''Couldn't it wait for a day or two?'' Her hand moved caressingly across his bare chest as her wide gray eyes pleaded with him not to leave her.

''I don't have any choice, honey,'' he said reluctantly, catching her hand in his. ''I have to leave right away. I'll only be gone for a few days at the most. When I come back, we'll talk this out.''

Mase showered and dressed, not even taking time for breakfast. They spoke very little on the drive back to town, but when they arrived at her apartment, he turned to her once again.

"I'm sorry I have to leave you like this, but I'll be back soon," he said. "I love you, Evie."

"Good-bye, Mase," she replied, turning to walk up the steps before he could see the tears glimmering in her eyes.

Inside her apartment, she leaned back against tne door, waiting for the sound of his departing pickup. Her little dream of love and security had just crumbled before her eyes.

Some men were born to be wanderers, she forced herself to admit, and Mase was obviously one of them. He had lived his life without putting down roots. She had been a fool to believe he would change for her sake.

The words he had spoken in the darkness of the night had carried a tantalizing hint of commitment, and for a short time she had allowed herself to believe them. But those words had been spoken in the heat of passion, and passion was a fleeting thing indeed. In the harsh light of day, Mase must have realized what he had done, and he'd fled in fear of that commitment.

Evie blinked furiously, trying to force back the tears that blurred her vision, but failing. Angry with herself, she brushed the dampness from her cheeks.

Mase had promised he would come back, she argued with herself, and she had no reason to doubt his word. He had never lied to her. But what would she do if he did return?

What if he expected her to give up her home and friends to share his rootless existence? Evie couldn't stand to live like that.

What was she going to do? She couldn't live the way Mase did, but she was beginning to fear that she couldn't live without him, either. At least here she had the stability and security she craved.

But not love. After finally having a taste of it, how could she go back to living without love?

There was a slight chance that she was pregnant. After their second night together, Mase had taken steps to protect her, and at the time she had appreciated his concern. Now she wished he had not taken those precautions. At least when he was gone she would have had his child to love.

The tears fell freely and she no longer tried to stop them. Evie lay down on her bed and curled up into a tight ball of misery. The future stretched out before her, long and lonely. The person who'd said it was better to have loved and lost than never to have loved at all didn't know what he was talking about. It would have been infinitely easier if she'd never known what she'd missed.

It was as if Mase had completed her, had taught her what it was to be whole. Now, without him, Evie felt emptier than she had ever felt in her life.

SEVENTEEN

Evie watched the festive merrymakers throughout the town with an air of quiet despair. She had cried for two hours that morning when she awoke to find positive proof that she was not pregnant. She was determined not to shed another tear. She had made her decision and she would have to learn to live with it.

Work had always been her solution when problems got her down. She tied back her hair and dressed in her oldest clothes, venturing downstairs to scrub the already immaculate kitchen floor. By noon she had finished that task and was busy washing the large windows at the front of the dining room.

She didn't realize how late it was until the kitchen crew started to arrive to begin work on that night's dinner. When she glanced around behind her, she found Ben watching her, a puzzled look on his face.

"I just washed those windows last week," he said. "Is something wrong with 'em?"

"There were just a few fingerprints," she explained guiltily.

"Anyway, since you're here, Liesel and I wanted to talk to you."

"Sure, Ben," she replied, a flicker of curiosity penetrating her depression. "Come on into my office."

Evie perched on the edge of her desk to give them space to stand in the tiny room. The older couple stood side by side, and Ben's hand rested comfortably on Liesel's shoulder.

"We vanted you to know first, Evie . . ." Liesel started. "Ben and I are going to be married."

"That's wonderful," Evie said after a moment of stunned surprise. "I'm very happy for both of you. When is the big day?"

"As soon as we can get together with Reverend Anderson," Ben said. "Probably right after the first of the year."

His eyes met Liesel's and the glow of their happiness filled their faces with a radiance that was ageless. Liesel looked like a girl of twenty again.

Of course she was happy for her friends, but Evie could not suppress the feeling of bittersweet regret that filled her heart. Was she destined never to know that kind of happiness firsthand?

"I hope this doesn't mean you'll be leaving me," she said at last.

"Nope. We seem to be pretty well settled here," Ben replied. "Uh, Evie . . . we were thinking. If things work out with . . . I mean, if you ever think of selling the restaurant, I've got some money put away . . ."

His voice faded when he saw the look on Evie's face. She fought valiantly to hold them back, but tears clouded her eyes.

"Of course," she said with forced cheerfulness. "I'll remember that. Now if you'll excuse me, I need to go change."

Her eyes were fastened firmly to the floor as she fled the room for the sanctuary of her lonely apartment.

Three days later, Mase returned to town. Evie saw his truck in front of the restaurant, and she could not repress the wave of happiness that washed over her. He had come back.

A moment later, that first rush of exultation receded, and she abruptly changed her mind about going out. She slipped back up the stairs and sat silently on the couch, waiting for the sound of his knock. She did not have long to wait.

It took all her self-control to keep from running to the door and throwing it open. She longed to feel his arms around her one last time, but she knew it was impossible. If she did, she would never be able to let him go.

The knocking stopped, and she heard the muffled sound of his footfalls as he went back down the stairs. It was only a temporary reprieve. That night she would have to face him and give the most difficult performance of her life. She had to convince Mase that she did not love him.

Evie was determined that tonight of all nights, Mase wouldn't have the advantage. She dressed carefully for the part. The sapphire-blue velvet dress she had donned was elegant and sophisticated but in no way provocative. Her hair was drawn back into a simple knot at the nape of her neck, and her makeup was even more discreet than usual.

Her eyes watched the door constantly all evening. The dinner rush was just coming to a close when she saw him appear in the entryway. Evie was struck anew by his overwhelming masculinity.

He was wearing the sweater that she had given him for Christmas, she noticed. His eyes fastened on her from across the room, roving proprietarily over her pleasantly rounded figure. His smile was warm and welcoming. It would be all too easy to succumb to its lure.

"Hi," she greeted him, her heart racing as she neared him.

"Hi, yourself."

"Have you eaten yet?"

"I had a sandwich this afternoon. It's not food that I'm interested in now."

"Oh, well, would you like to have something to drink? I really can't leave this early."

"Go ahead, Evie," Ben encouraged her. "I can take over here. It hasn't been very busy tonight, anyway."

"Uh, I suppose I could," she hesitated. "Thanks, Ben. Give me a call if you need me for anything."

Mase's arm encircled her shoulders, holding her along the length of his hard body. Leaden feet carried her slowly up the stairs to her apartment. As the door closed behind them, his smile encompassed her, luring her toward him with its unspoken promise. He caught her shoulders and tried to draw her closer, but she pulled away.

"Please don't, Mase," she pleaded. "This is going to be hard enough as it is."

"What's wrong, Evie?" he asked, his face reflecting his confusion. "Did something happen while I was gone?"

"No, nothing happened, really. I just did a lot of thinking about us."

"What is there to think about? We love each other and we're going to get married."

"No, Mase, we're not."

"What?"

"You heard me," she said staunchly.

"Sure, I heard you. I just can't believe you said it. Evie, I love you."

"I know you do," she replied as gently as she could. "And I'm sorry, but I don't love you."

He searched her face, willing her to relent and admit her love for him, but Evie did not waver. After a moment his expression changed and a glint of anger appeared in his deep green eyes.

"So you've decided to go back to playing Sleeping Beauty," he observed tightly. "I guess you'd rather sleep your life away in your safe, lonely tower than take a chance on life with a flesh and blood man. Think about it, Evie. Think hard about what we have together. Don't throw our love away because you're afraid."

He gripped her chin and forced her face up to meet his. Her eyes reluctantly rose, and the look of wounded desperation that she found in his filled her with such pain that it took her breath away.

"I'm sorry, Mase," she repeated helplessly. "Please believe that I never meant to hurt you. I wish things could have been different."

"Why are you doing this, Evie?" he demanded. "I know you're lying. I know that you love me."

His strong arms pulled her forcefully against him, and his lips took hers in a bruising, demanding kiss. His tongue speared boldly between her lips, claiming every inch of warm, wet, welcoming flesh as his property. He felt a shudder ripple through her body, and she went limp, giving herself up fully to his embrace.

Evie tried to imprint everything about him—the feel, the taste, the musky, totally masculine smell of his hard body—indelibly in her memory. In that way at least she would carry a part of him with her for the rest of her life.

An eternity later, their lips parted and Mase's crushing hold on her loosened. The impulse to forget her decision and stay in the shelter of his arms was nearly too much for her resolve. She had to force herself to pull away from him.

"I knew it," he murmured with satisfaction. "I knew you felt the same way."

"No, Mase," she replied, the finality of her tone chilling him. "I won't deny that you can make me respond physically, but that doesn't mean I love you. Desire isn't enough. I'm sorry."

EIGHTEEN

The next morning Evie dressed and went down to work as usual, hoping to lose herself in the comfortable routine that had been her life for so long. Her strategy worked to a point, but nothing could truly erase the image of Mase from her mind.

The only thing that managed to capture and hold her attention was the door of the restaurant. Every time it opened, her eyes flew to it, half expecting to see Mase standing there, but this time she knew for certain that he would not be there. It was over.

Evie lay in bed the morning of New Year's Eve, thinking about the coming evening. It would bring an end to the holiday festivities at last. She only hoped that she could survive the celebration she had planned to share with Mase.

The morning was spent in decorating the restaurant. Pine boughs and glittery balls were replaced with streamers and balloons, and the only reminder of Christmas was the huge tree that stood beside the piano.

It was nearly time to open before Evie escaped to her apartment for a short time to change into the slinky black dress she had bought two weeks earlier. It clung discreetly to every curve of her body, the neckline dipping just low enough to display an enticing hint of cleavage and the slim line of her back exposed to the waist.

She thought briefly of how Mase would have reacted to the sight of her in this gown, and a lump formed in her throat. She sat down on the edge of the bed and raised her skirt to put on her sheer stockings, trying to shut out the provocative pictures her mind produced.

A delicate silver necklace and bracelet and strappy sandals completed her ensemble. She applied a bit of lipstick and hurried downstairs.

"Oh, Evie," Liesel called from near the front door. "Do you vant us to reserve a table for you?"

"I won't be needing a table."

"But where will Mase sit? If he doesn't arrive early, dere may not be a table left."

"Mase won't be coming tonight," Evie replied, her voice choked with tears. "I won't be seeing him again."

She turned and fled to her office, her chest heaving with silent sobs as she fought for control. A moment later, Liesel followed her.

"Vat is vong, liebling?" Liesel asked compassionately, her arm encircling the younger woman's bare, trembling shoulders. "You and Mase haf had a fight?"

"Not a fight. Not really. Oh, Liesel, I'm such a coward. Mase asked me to marry him, but I can't. I just can't live the way he does . . . the way I *did* when I was a child. My life here is the first security I've ever had. I can't give it up. Breaking up with Mase was my decision. I should be relieved that everything is back to normal, but instead, I've never been so miserable in my life."

Her pent-up tears escaped her iron control and ran in rivulets down her cheeks.

"Evie dear, you are very confused. Ve haf been together for a long time. I know you vell, perhaps better than you know yourself. You did not break up with Mase because you don't vant to leave Leavenworth. It is because you are afraid. Don't let that fear rule your life. The only security dere really is comes from loving someone and from being loved. In the end, that is all that really matters. Think about how you felt ven you were with Mase. Search your heart, Evie. It will tell you vat you must do."

Liesel left without another word, and Evie sat at her desk, contemplating the older woman's words. Could she really go back to living her life as she had before she met Mase?

Everything she did, everywhere she went, she was reminded of him. She missed his companionship, his laughing green eyes, his teasing, the smell of his woodsy, masculine cologne.

Her newly awakened body missed the touch of his hands and the feel of his hard, throbbing manhood filling her and taking her to the peak of ecstasy. But most of all, she missed the simple happiness and security she had always felt when he enfolded her in his massive embrace.

Mase had said that he loved her, and Evie now faced the fact that she was hopelessly and irrevocably in love with him. She thought back to Mase's angry words and found an element of truth in them. She *had* been afraid.

Evie knew there was no reason to think he would hurt her. She had thought about it over and over, but it was one thing to reason it out dispassionately and another thing altogether to believe it with her emotions.

She had lived in the shadow of fear since her childhood. In that way she had allowed Kyle Richards to exile her to a life of lonely solitude. She was still allowing him to control her life.

But no longer, she told herself, leaping decisively to her feet. For the first time in her life, Evie had found something worth taking a chance on. She would step out of the shadows and into the sunlight of love. She only hoped it was not too late.

Without a word to anyone, Evie grabbed her coat and purse and ran out to her car. It was snowing and the roads were slick, but she didn't care. Nothing was more important than being with Mase.

She forced herself to drive slowly, traversing the icy curves outside town with caution. The snow swirled around the car with a rhythm that was hypnotic, and she had to force herself to concentrate on the road.

The miles separating them passed slowly, and as she neared the cabin, her foot unconsciously pressed down harder on the accelerator. As she rounded a curve, her headlights illuminated the huge form of a tree sprawled across the road before her. Evie began pumping furiously at the brakes, and somehow she managed to bring her car safely to a halt.

She sat for a moment, shocked but grateful for her close escape. When her trembling subsided, she eased herself out of the car to survey the problem.

The thick tree trunk had effectively blocked the road, she was forced to admit. There was no way to get around it. Her face was set with determination. She had not come this far only to turn back. Luckily, it was not far to the cabin.

Mase sat in the huge, elegant living room and stared moodily into the fire. He really should be in the bedroom packing, he told himself. He wanted to get an early start for Seattle in the morning. He had started to walk down the hall several times, but he had always come back. The room held too many memories of Evie.

Was he giving up too easily? He loved Evie, and he was convinced that she loved him, too. Her rejection had hurt him deeply, but he knew she had done it out of fear.

What was she so desperately afraid of? Surely not of him. If he hadn't proved by now that he would never hurt her, then nothing he could do would convince her. There had to be some other reason.

Mase reached out for the half-empty glass of bourbon that sat on the table beside him. He had lifted it just a few inches off the table when the sharp sound of a knock on the door echoed through the cabin.

When he went to the door and opened it cautiously, he was stunned to find Evie standing there. She looked half frozen, very much the way she had the night he'd met her. Without speaking, he grabbed her arm and pulled her inside, slamming the door behind them.

"Are you trying to kill yourself?" he asked roughly. "Or do you just enjoy frostbite?"

"A tree w-was down across the road," she stammered, shivering uncontrollably. "It wasn't m-my fault."

"It never is."

Mase swept her up in his arms and carried her into the warmth of the living room. He settled her carefully on the couch, as if fearful she would break.

Evie watched him tenderly as he unbuttoned her coat and slid it off. He looked terrible. Why did that fact suddenly make her heart feel lighter?

When he knelt before her to take off her shoes, a dark scowl marred his face. He unbuckled the slender straps and slid them off numb feet.

"Why the hell didn't you wear boots?" he roared, settling one icy little foot between his warm thighs. "It'll be a miracle if you really *don't* have frostbite."

His big hands enclosed the other foot, not massaging it but simply allowing the heat of his flesh to warm hers. Evie sat silently under his ministrations, shivering so violently that she couldn't have spoken if her life had depended on it.

After a few minutes of contact with Mase's warmth, feeling began to return to her feet. First they tingled and then they started to hurt. As if aware of the fact, Mase released them and rose.

"I'll be right back. Don't move."

A few minutes later he was back. His hands pulled her to a sitting position and he fumbled behind her for the fastening of her dress. He quickly dispensed with it and went on to her skimpy underclothes.

"Mase, I don't—"

"Shut up," he barked in his best drill sergeant voice. "You've pushed me too far, Evie. One more word and I'll turn you over my knee and blister your bottom."

Evie shut up. When she was stripped to the skin, Mase stood and picked her up in his arms, striding down the hall toward the bedroom. He did not stop by the bed but walked over to the steaming hot tub and carefully settled her on the seat.

The shock of the warm, churning water made her gasp, but she soon relaxed and leaned back against the hard marble side. Her eyes closed and she sighed with pleasure.

Mase hovered close to her, waiting for the heated water to do its job. Excitement pulsed through his body, driving out the depression that had been his companion for the past few days. She had come back!

He glanced down and saw the warm flush that suffused her skin. Her trembling had stopped and the sight of her breasts beneath the bubbling water tantalized him.

"Mase, please don't be angry with me," she begged. "I had to see you. I stayed away as long as I could. You were right, you know. I *do* love you. I was just afraid to admit it to you, or to myself."

"Why, Evie?" he asked, going still.

"It was because of the way you live. I didn't think I could live that way, traveling all the time, with no real home. Because of Kyle, that was how I lived all through my childhood.

"For a long time now, this town, my business, my home have all meant security to me. I didn't think I could be happy without them. Then tonight someone made me realize something I should have known all along. Do you know what security is to me? It's feeling comfortable and safe, and being happy. And do you know what? I realized that's how I feel when I'm with you. It isn't my home, or my business, or even my family. I feel secure when I'm with *you*, because I love you, Mase, and I know that you love me and that you'll never hurt me. I'm not afraid any longer. If you still want me, I'll go anywhere with you."

"If I still want you?" Mase repeated incredulously. "I'll want you till the day I die. My life would be nothing without you."

Still completely dressed, Mase stepped into the tub with her, drawing her into a fierce embrace. Their lips met, and for a time they were content to simply hold each other, their tongues playing seductive little lovers' games.

Evie's fingers went to the buttons of his flannel shirt, slowly easing them out of their holes, one by one, caressing the warm, wet skin beneath. When she reached the zipper of his jeans, Mase raised his hips off the seat to allow her to slide them off. The wet denim was stubborn and it took both their efforts to dispose of them.

Naked at last, he sat down on the bench and pulled Evie astride his lap, facing him. Her full, rosy breasts were in line with his mouth, just as he had intended them to be. He teased the tender flesh with his lips and tongue.

He entered her swiftly, plunging deeply and fully into her welcoming softness. The pleasure was more intense, more fulfilling, more perfect, than it had ever been before. They were together every step of the way, and as the waves of ecstasy washed over them, they clung to each other as if they would never again let go.

Finally Mase stirred. Evie's head turned on his shoulder and she looked up at him with soft, trusting eyes. His head lowered to seek hers, and when their lips met, it was more than a mere kiss that they exchanged. It was a promise. A vow.

"You know, love," Mase said. "As much as I'd like to stay just like this for the rest of our lives, I think maybe we'd better get out of this tub."

"Why?" Evie asked, rubbing against him with the tactile pleasure of a cat, enjoying the feel of his slick, wet skin.

"Aside from the fact that pretty soon we're both going to look like prunes, we have to consider the possibility of drowning."

"But what a way to go," she quipped happily.

The slap he delivered to her bare fanny lost a good deal of its force under water, but Evie got the message. She eased herself up off him and they stepped out of the tub.

Using towels he had left on the railing, they dried every inch of each other's bodies. They both knew they should settle matters between them before the night was out. If only the bed had not been so close, they might have made it back to the living room. As it was, they simply didn't have a chance.

Although they were both tired from several sleepless nights, it was far into the morning hours before they fell asleep.

_____ NINETEEN _____

Evie awoke to bright sunshine. Glancing across their shared pillow, she found that Mase was still deeply asleep.

There was no chance that she could go back to sleep, for not only was she too impatiently, vibrantly awake, she was also too hungry. Now that she thought of it, she hadn't eaten since yesterday morning when Liesel had bullied her into eating a piece of toast.

She slipped out of bed, being careful not to wake Mase. She had a feeling that they would both need a good meal to fortify them for the discussion to come.

Mase turned in his sleep and reached out for Evie. Unable to find her, he sat straight up in bed, brought to instant alertness. Had he only dreamed that she was here with him?

His eyes searched the room and found their towels still lying on the floor where they had dropped them the night before. He breathed a sigh of relief.

He rolled out of bed and went to look in the bathroom, but there was no sign of her there. He moved on to the living room, which was also deserted, but he detected the scent of fresh coffee.

From his vantage point in the doorway, Mase observed Evie without being seen. He couldn't help a smile at the sight of her dressed in one of his shirts. The hem fell almost to her knees, and the sleeves had been rolled up many times to get the cuffs above her hands.

Her long hair fell loose around her shoulders and down her back, swaying slightly as her slim, bare feet kept time to some music that was heard only in her head. A satisfied smile turned his lips upward.

Evie stepped up onto a chair that stood next to her, reaching into a cupboard for a canister of sugar. Mase crept up silently behind her. He slid a brawny arm around her waist and pulled her off the chair, holding her firmly against him. She let out a startled shriek and clutched at his arm.

"Mase, you fiend. Put me down this minute."

He set her down, and she turned to face him. A soft pink flush colored her cheeks at the sight of his naked, aroused body. His hands rested lightly on the collar of the shirt she wore. Without warning, he gripped the fabric and gave it a sharp tug. Buttons went flying to all corners of the big kitchen.

"You were wearing too many clothes," he explained, as if it were the most natural thing in the world.

"There's no satisfying some men," Evie pouted.

"Last night you were complaining that I didn't wear enough."

"It *is* a bit different when you're out walking in a snowstorm, honey. But as for not satisfying *some* men, you definitely satisfy *me*, and you won't ever have to worry about any other man."

He bent down to kiss her, and Evie wound her arms around his neck. Their lips met and Mase straightened up, lifting Evie off the floor.

"I suppose now is as good a time as any to have that talk," he said when they came up for breath.

"It might be easier if you put me down," Evie suggested, her fingers toying with the soft hair on the back of his head. "It's hard to be serious this way."

"Being serious is vastly overrated," he commented, his hands tickling the base of her spine. "We can talk just as easily this way."

He walked out into the living room and sat on the couch, taking Evie with him. They cuddled comfortably on the soft velour expanse, Evie's head resting on his shoulder.

"You're very sure that you love me?" he questioned, needing to hear the words.

"I'm sure, Mase." She raised her head to look him in the eye. "I really knew it all along. It was just my silly common sense that made me hesitate."

"I know how much your home means to you. Are you sure you'd be willing to give it up for me?"

"I already have, Mase. Ben and Liesel are getting married and they want to buy my restaurant. I'm going to sell it to them. I don't need it now. As long as we're together, anywhere we go will be home.''

The look on his face puzzled her, and her fingers caressed his brow softly, trying to smooth away the unaccustomed furrows she found there.

''Mase? Is there something you're not telling me?''

''Yes,'' he admitted guiltily. ''I'm sorry, honey, but after what you put me through these last few days, I just needed a little reassurance.''

Evie's arms tightened around him.

''I wish you'd told me how you felt from the beginning, because all this wouldn't have been necessary.''

''What do you mean?'' Her eyes flew to his face.

Mase sighed and dipped his head until their foreheads touched. He paused for a moment, enjoying the simple physical contact before he continued.

''First maybe I should tell you a little bit about myself,'' he said softly. ''When I was a kid, I didn't have your typical *Leave It To Beaver* kind of family, either. My folks fought all the time. My dad had plenty of girlfriends on the side, and my mother, well . . . she had 'outside interests,' too. Neither of them had much time for me, and I grew up pretty wild. When I was fourteen, I got into some real trouble and wound up in juvenile detention. My parents were ready to leave me to rot, when Gramps stepped in and took me to live

live with him. I've never known a tougher, more demanding man in my life, but underneath it all, he really cared about me. He turned my life around," he said with a simplicity that did not hide the affection in his voice. "I shaped up, finished school, and after graduation, I joined the Army. That was sixteen years ago. About a month ago, Gramps died. I had quite a bit of leave coming, so I came home to arrange things and also to think about my future."

Evie pressed closer, wordlessly offering him comfort. He accepted it gratefully, hugging her warm, yielding body against his own.

"For a long time I thought the Army was all I needed," he continued at last. "But lately it seemed like something was missing from my life. I didn't realize what it was until I met you."

"Me?" she asked, genuinely puzzled.

"Yes, you," he replied, a tender look banishing his sadness. "You made me realize that I needed someone to share my life and my dreams with. I hate going home at night to an empty apartment, but I got tired of the singles scene a long time ago. I'm tired of turning on the television just to hear the sound of a human voice. I was so afraid that you were going to send me back to that empty life I had before I met you. I know how much you love this town, and to be honest, I've gotten kind of fond of it myself. When I went out of town, I resigned my commission. All I want now is to settle down in one place, with you. Do you remember the day we saw that old ski lodge outside town?"

"Sure, I remember, but what—"

"Shh," he hushed her with a finger across her lips. "Let me finish.

"Well, with your experience in the restaurant business and my experience, uh . . . giving orders, I thought we could make a go of it. I left town when I did to close the deal. It's ours now. We can restore it and make it into the best winter resort in the state. It'll take a lot of hard work, but I think we can do it."

"It sounds wonderful, but Mase . . ." she hesitated.

"Hmm?"

"Are you sure this is what you want? The Army has been your whole life. I don't want you to feel like I trapped you into giving it up."

"I'm doing it because I want to, Evie," he assured her. "I think that all those years I spent wandering I was really looking for something. I found that something the night I came across a half-frozen little waif in the middle of a blizzard. It just took me a while to realize it. Neither of us had much of a childhood. It will be different for our children. They'll have all the security and stability that we can give them."

"And love," Evie added, teardrops glistening in her silvery gray eyes.

"And love," Mase agreed, drawing her still closer.

In Mase's arms, Evie knew that what she had waited for all her life was finally hers. Her winter dream of love had become a reality.